出版説明

　　本館一向倡導優質閱讀，近年來連續推出了以 "Q" 為標識的 "Quality English Learning 優質英語學習" 系列，其中《讀名著學英語》叢書，更是香港書展入選好書，讀者反響令人鼓舞。推動社會閱讀風氣，推動英語經典閱讀，藉閱讀拓廣世界視野，提高英語水平，已經成為一種潮流。

　　然良好閱讀習慣的養成非一日之功，大多數初、中級程度的讀者，常視直接閱讀厚重的原著為畏途。如何給年輕的讀者提供切實的指引和幫助，如何既提供優質的學習素材，又提供名師的教學方法，是當下社會關注的重要問題。針對這種情況，本館特別延請香港名校名師，根據多年豐富的教學經驗，精選海外適合初、中級英語程度讀者的優質經典讀物，有系統地出版了這套叢書，名為《Black Cat 優質英語階梯閱讀》。

　　《Black Cat 優質英語階梯閱讀》體現了香港名校名師堅持經典學習的教學理念，以及多年行之有效的學習方法。既有經過改寫和縮寫的經典名著，又有富創意的現代作品；既有精心設計的聽、説、讀、寫綜合練習，又有豐富的歷史文化知識；既有彩色插圖、繪圖和照片，又有英美專業演員朗讀作品的 CD。適合口味不同的讀者享受閱讀之樂，欣賞經典之美。

　　《Black Cat 優質英語階梯閱讀》由淺入深，逐階提升，好像參與一個尋寶遊戲，入門並不難，但要真正尋得寶藏，需要投入，更需要堅持。只有置身其中的人，才能體味純正英語的魅力，領略得到真寶的快樂。當英語閱讀成為自己生活的一部分，英語水平的提高自然水到渠成。

商務印書館 (香港) 有限公司

編輯部

使用説明 _____

① 應該怎樣選書？

按閱讀興趣選書

《Black Cat 優質英語階梯閱讀》精選世界經典作品，也包括富於創意的現代作品；既有膾炙人口的小説、戲劇，又有非小説類的文化知識讀物，品種豐富，內容多樣，適合口味不同的讀者挑選自己感興趣的書，享受閱讀的樂趣。

按英語程度選書

《Black Cat 優質英語階梯閱讀》現設 Level 1 至 Level 6，由淺入深，涵蓋初、中級英語程度。讀物分級採用了國際上通用的劃分標準，主要以詞彙（vocabulary）和結構（structures）劃分。

Level 1 至 Level 3 出現的詞彙較淺顯，相對深的核心詞彙均配上中文解釋，節省讀者查找詞典的時間，以專心理解正文內容。在註釋的幫助下，讀者若能流暢地閱讀正文內容，就不用擔心這一本書程度過深。

Level 1 至 Level 3 出現的動詞時態形式和句子結構比較簡單。動詞時態形式以現在時（present simple）、現在時進行式（present continuous）、過去時（past simple）為主，句子結構大部分是簡單句（simple sentences）。此外，還包括比較級和最高級（comparative and superlative forms）、可數和不可數名詞（countable and uncountable nouns）以及冠詞（articles）等語法知識點。

Level 4 至 Level 6 出現的動詞時態形式，以現在完成時（present perfect）、現在完成時進行式（present perfect continuous）、過去完成時（past perfect continuous）為主，句子結構大部分是複合句（compound sentences）、條件從句（1st and 2nd conditional sentences）等。此外，還包括情態動詞（modal verbs）、被動形式（passive forms）、動名詞（gerunds）、

The Big Mistake
and Other Stories

奇情故事

商務印書館

Name of Book: The Big Mistake and Other Stories
Author: Bruna Deriu
Activities and footnotes: Nella Burnett-Stuart
Editor: Rosalba Foreman
Design: Nadia Maestri
Illustrations: Mario Benvenuto, Enzo Marciante, Nicola Rovetta
Edition: ©2003 Black Cat Publishing
         an imprint of Cideb Editrice, Genoa, Canterbury

系 列 名：Black Cat 優質英語階梯閱讀 · Level 5
書　　名：奇情故事
責任編輯：黃淑嫻
封面設計：張　毅　曹　磊
出　　版：商務印書館（香港）有限公司
　　　　　香港筲箕灣耀興道 3 號東滙廣場 8 樓
　　　　　http://www.commercialpress.com.hk
發　　行：香港聯合書刊物流有限公司
　　　　　香港新界大埔汀麗路 36 號中華商務印刷大廈 3 字樓
印　　刷：中華商務彩色印刷有限公司
　　　　　香港新界大埔汀麗路 36 號中華商務印刷大廈
版　　次：2013 年 5 月第 1 版第 3 次印刷
　　　　　© 商務印書館（香港）有限公司
　　　　　ISBN 978 962 07 1659 1
　　　　　Printed in Hong Kong

短語動詞（phrasal verbs）等語法知識點。

　　根據上述的語法範圍，讀者可按自己實際的英語水平，如詞彙量、語法知識、理解能力、閱讀能力等自主選擇，不再受制於學校年級劃分或學歷高低的約束，完全根據個人需要選擇合適的讀物。

② 怎樣提高閱讀效果？

　　閱讀的方法主要有兩種：一是泛讀，二是精讀。兩者各有功能，適當地結合使用，相輔相成，有事半功倍之效。

　　泛讀，指閱讀大量適合自己程度（可稍淺，但不能過深）、不同內容、風格、體裁的讀物，但求明白內容大意，不用花費太多時間鑽研細節，主要作用是多接觸英語，減輕對它的生疏感，鞏固以前所學過的英語，讓腦子在潛意識中吸收詞彙用法、語法結構等。

　　精讀，指小心認真地閱讀內容精彩、組織有條理、遣詞造句又正確的作品，着重點在於理解 "準確" 及 "深入"，欣賞其精彩獨到之處。精讀時，可充分利用書中精心設計的練習，學習掌握有用的英語詞彙和語法知識。精讀後，可再花十分鐘朗讀其中一小段有趣的文字，邊唸邊細心領會文字的結構和意思。

　　《Black Cat 優質英語階梯閱讀》中的作品均值得精讀，如時間有限，不妨嘗試每兩個星期泛讀一本，輔以每星期挑選書中一章精彩的文字精讀。要學好英語，持之以恆地泛讀和精讀英文是最有效的方法。

③ 本系列的練習與測試有何功能？

　　《Black Cat 優質英語階梯閱讀》特別注重練習的設計，為讀者考慮周到，切合實用需求，學習功能強。每章後均配有訓練聽、說、讀、寫四項技能的練習，分量、難度恰到好處。

聽力練習分兩類，一是重聽故事回答問題，二是聆聽主角對話、書信朗讀、或模擬記者訪問後寫出答案，旨在以生活化的練習形式逐步提高聽力。每本書均配有 CD 提供作品朗讀，朗讀者都是專業演員，英國作品由英國演員錄音，美國作品由美國演員錄音，務求增加聆聽的真實感和感染力。多聆聽英式和美式英語兩種發音，可讓讀者熟悉二者的差異，逐漸培養分辨英美發音的能力，提高聆聽理解的準確度。此外，模仿錄音朗讀故事或模仿主人翁在戲劇中的對白，都是訓練口語能力的好方法。

閱讀理解練習形式多樣化，有縱橫字謎、配對、填空、字句重組等等，注重訓練讀者的理解、推敲和聯想等多種閱讀技能。

寫作練習尤具新意，教讀者使用網式圖示（spidergrams）記錄重點，採用問答、書信、電報、記者採訪等多樣化形式，鼓勵讀者動手寫作。

書後更設有升級測試（Exit Test）及答案，供讀者檢查學習效果。充分利用書中的練習和測試，可全面提升聽、說、讀、寫四項技能。

④ 本系列還能提供甚麼幫助？

《Black Cat 優質英語階梯閱讀》提倡豐富多元的現代閱讀，巧用書中提供的資訊，有助於提升英語理解力，擴闊視野。

每本書都設有專章介紹相關的歷史文化知識，經典名著更有作者生平、社會背景等資訊。書內富有表現力的彩色插圖、繪圖和照片，使閱讀充滿趣味，部分加上如何解讀古典名畫的指導，增長見識。有的書還提供一些與主題相關的網址，比如關於不同國家的節慶源流的網址，讓讀者多利用網上資源增進知識。

Contents

Four stories are recorded. 故事選錄

This symbol indicates the stories featured on the
accompanying CD. 故事的錄音標記

A Case of Trust

The Penfriend

The Big Mistake

Marge and Olive

Simpson's Buried Treasure

A Strange Case

A CasE
of Trust

Before reading

1 **Look at the words in the box and decide which job is:**

- the most exciting ....
- the most interesting ....
- the most difficult ....
- the most well-paid ....
- the most dangerous ....

> teacher   plumber [1]   policeman   detective   lawyer
> builder   lorry driver   miner   politician
> accountant   nurse   librarian   butler [2]   artist

Which job would you like to do? Why?

....

Which job you wouldn't like to do? Why?

....

2 **Look at the list below:**

Parts of the body: ....

Food: ....

Weather: ....

Furniture: ....

Buildings: ....

Now read the story and find words that go into each category.

1. **plumber** : a person whose job is to repair water-pipes or water-tanks.
2. **butler** : chief male servant of the house.

A CaSE

of Trust

The tall man in uniform knocked nervously [1] on the office door. Detective Miller wanted to see him but he had no idea why. The door opened. Miller smiled and beckoned [2] with his hand.

'Come in,' he said, closing the door behind them.   5

'John Baker, sir.' The younger man said.

'Yes. I know who you are. Relax, don't be so nervous!' Miller replied. 'Sit down'.

'Thank you, sir.'

Baker was worried. It was the first time that Miller had   10
called him to his office. He sat down, hoping there was
nothing wrong. Miller sat opposite him. There was silence for

---

1. **nervously** : worriedly and anxiously.
2. **beckoned** : signalled, indicated.

a few seconds. After a while, Miller cleared his throat and
spoke.

15 'Listen, Baker. The head office has asked me for a list of my
best men. They want to promote somebody in this office.'

Baker sat forward on his chair.

'Promotion, sir?' he asked.

'Yes, Baker. I'm thinking of giving them your name.

20 'Thank you, sir,' Baker replied excitedly.

'Don't thank me yet. I've heard good things about you. Your
colleagues [1] call you "the brain" – I presume [2] it's because of
your intelligence...' Miller said, opening the drawer in his
desk. Baker shrugged [3] his shoulders modestly. Miller took a

25 folder [4] out of the drawer and handed it to him.

'Read this,' he said, staring at the desk in front of him as he
spoke. 'It's a strange case – see what you can make of it. [5] Take
it with you. When you've solved it, bring it back. Don't forget
that your promotion could depend on the solution!'

30 Miller stood up and Baker realized that it was time for him
to go. He thanked Miller and left the office cheerfully. He
looked quickly at the clock and saw that it was almost
midday. Time for his lunch-break. Good. He could read the
case, and hopefully solve it by the end of the day. The

35 promotion would soon be his.

1. **colleagues** : group of people who work in the same company.
2. **presume** : suppose to be true.
3. **shrugged** : lifted (his shoulders).
4. **folder** : folded piece of card used for holding papers.
5. **see what you can make of it** : see if you can understand it.

As usual, his desk was untidy. He pushed the papers to one side to make room [1] for his sandwiches. He connected the telephone answering machine, so as not to be disturbed. Then, he opened the folder, and began to read the contents:

40 'William Cranberry woke up with a strange idea in mind. He wanted to go to the public library but couldn't understand why. He'd never been there before and his own personal library was full of books that he had never read. He told his butler, Jenkins, of his plans and after breakfast, Jenkins took 45 the car out of the garage.[2] They drove to the library and William Cranberry went in alone. As he walked around the bookshelves, he was approached [3] by a librarian. She asked if he was looking for anything in particular. Without thinking, William Cranberry asked for *Strange Destiny*,[4] by a certain 50 B. Dale. He didn't know why he had asked for that particular book as he had never heard of it before. The librarian moved away and then came back with a small book. William Cranberry took it and thanked her. When he opened the book, a piece of paper fell to the floor.

55 He picked it up and read it. It was a receipt [5] from the local pawnshop.[6] Somebody had left it in the book. William

1. **make room** : make space.
2. **garage** : car-park.
3. **approached** : came near.
4. **destiny** : fate.
5. **receipt** : written piece of paper which states something has been paid.
6. **pawnshop** : a shop that lends money in exchange for expensive items left there.

Cranberry was a curious man – he wanted to know what had been pawned. He left the library immediately and went to see the pawnbroker. [1] He gave in the receipt and bought back the pawned item. It was a small antique, [2] silver mirror that was probably worth [3] a lot of money. William Cranberry was pleased with his purchase. He took it home and cleaned it carefully. As he was cleaning it, he noticed that the handle was loose. [4] He unscrewed [5] the handle and found a visiting card inside. He read the card:

> **Madame Eve, Clairvoyant.** [6]
> **10 Rosehip Lane**
> **London SW6**

William Cranberry had a problem. His business was not going well – he had lost a lot of money due to a careless investment. He had never been to see a clairvoyant before so perhaps she could give him some good advice. Besides, the series of coincidences [7] that had made him find the visiting

---

1. **pawnbroker** : person to whom people bring expensive items (a pawn) so that he will lend them money. If the money is not repaid within a certain time he can sell the items. A pawnbroker works in a pawnshop.
2. **antique** : very old.
3. **worth** : has the value of.
4. **loose** : not firmly fixed.
5. **unscrewed** : removed the screws (a 'screw' is similar to a nail).
6. **clairvoyant** : person who is able to see in the future.
7. **coincidences** : occasions when similar things happen at the same time.

card meant that fate wanted him to go there. Without telling anyone, he made an appointment [1] with Madame Eve.

He found the house easily. Madame Eve opened the door. Cranberry was expecting to see a strange woman wearing eccentric [2] clothes and carrying a crystal ball. Madame Eve, however, looked very ordinary – middle-aged and very serious. She showed him into an empty room. There were only two small wooden chairs for them to sit on. She explained that she was changing the furniture, and that she was waiting for the delivery [3] that evening.

Cranberry was sure that he had never seen her before in his life, yet she knew everything about him. Even private things. She knew about his old girlfriends, she described his home and gave details of his childhood. William Cranberry was amazed because he had never believed in such things. He wanted to know more and at the end of his visit, she gave him the advice he asked for. She told him that his bad luck was caused by a jealous spirit. To free himself of this bad luck, he had to take his most expensive heirloom [4] and bury [5] it in his mother's grave [6] for three days. Within three days his luck would change for the better.

75

80

85

90

---

1. **appointment** : meeting.
2. **eccentric** : strange.
3. **for the delivery** : for the furniture to be brought to the house.
4. **heirloom** : valuable possessions belonging to his ancestors.
5. **bury** : put it under the ground.
6. **grave** : place in the ground where a dead person is buried.

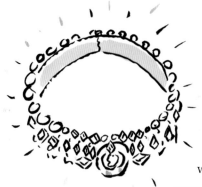

This is what William Cranberry did. He took the diamond necklace that had belonged to his great-grandmother, out of the safe. [1] It was very old, and was worth thousands of pounds. He wrapped it carefully in a black cloth, and put it into a plastic bag. Wearing old and torn [2] clothes, he went to the cemetery [3] after dark. He made sure that there was nobody around and then buried the necklace.

Unfortunately for William, things went from bad to worse over the next few days. He lost more money on the stock exchange [4] and caught the flu. [5] Then his butler, Jenkins went away for a few days; his mother was very ill, and he wanted to see her before she died. William Cranberry's luck had not changed at all. On the fourth day, he returned to the cemetery. Once again, he dug up his mother's grave. He couldn't find the necklace. He dug even deeper, but it was useless. Someone had stolen it! Annoyed with himself for his stupidity, he went to see Madame Eve. To his surprise and anger, Madame Eve had disappeared. The house was empty, and he had no way of

---

1. **safe** : usually a metal box in which money and valuables are kept.
2. **torn** : his clothes were in pieces.
3. **cemetery** : piece of land used for burying dead people.
4. **stock exchange** : place where stocks and shares are publicly bought and sold.
5. **flu** : bad cold.

finding her. He suspected that she was responsible but he didn't know how to prove it. He didn't want to ruin [1] his reputation [2] so he decided not to report it to the police. He tried to forget the incident.

115

Who stole the necklace? How did Madame Eve know about his past history? Why did William Cranberry want to go to the library?'

120

Baker finished his lunch, and closed the folder. He had read the story carefully, and had already solved the mystery. [3] He would soon be promoted, and all for a few minutes' work! He put a piece of paper into his typewriter, and began to type out his answer:

125

'Madame Eve had learned about William's life from her accomplice, [4] the butler. They had planned the theft together. The butler had hidden a small microphone in William Cranberry's pillow. [5] At night, a cassette-recording would repeat the orders, 'Go to the library, ask for *Strange Destiny*.' In the morning Cranberry remembered the orders without knowing why. The butler knew that Cranberry was a curious man and would not be able to resist a pawnbroker's receipt. He also knew that he had lost a lot of money, and would do anything to improve his business affairs. The clairvoyant convinced him that she could see the future, because she knew everything about his past. Her house was already empty and, together with the butler, they had already planned their

130

135

---

1. **ruin** : spoil or destroy.
2. **reputation** : the degree to which a person is trusted or admired.
3. **mystery** : something strange or unknown.
4. **accomplice** : a person who helps someone else to do illegal things.

5. **pillow** :

escape. He did not suspect her at all, and took her advice
140 without hesitation.'[1]

Baker put his written answer on top of the folder and
headed back [2] to Miller's office. He knocked and entered.

'Already?' Miller exclaimed.

'Yes, Sir.' Baker replied proudly.

145 Miller opened the folder and re-read the story. Then he
read Baker's reply. During this time Baker sat silently.
Suddenly Miller began to laugh, and he shook his head
disbelievingly. [3]

'Who'd have thought!' he cried. 'Well done, Baker. You've
150 certainly lived up to [4] your reputation!'

'Thank you, sir.'

Miller put the folder back into the drawer of his desk. He
stood and accompanied Baker to the door.

'Don't come to work tomorrow. Take a week's holiday. When
155 you return next Monday, you'll hear about the promotion.'

'Thank you, sir,' Baker replied.

He left the office and thought of the promotion for the rest of
the day. When he got home, he told his wife about it. She was
pleased, and insisted [5] on celebrating the event. They took some
160 of their savings out of the bank, and went abroad for five days.

1. **hesitation** : indecision.
2. **headed back** : returned.
3. **disbelievingly** : not believing.
4. **lived up to** : reached the standard that was expected.
5. **insisted** : demanded forcefully.

A CaꜱE of Trust

Monday morning soon arrived, and Baker returned to work. He wanted to see Miller. He went to the office and knocked on the door. He opened it and went in, but Miller wasn't there. A man was sitting at his desk.

'Yes?' The man looked up. 165

'Umm, I was looking for Detective Miller, sir,' Baker replied.

'I've taken his place. [1] You must be John Baker. Is there something I can do for you?'

'No, that's alright, thank you,' Baker replied.

He left the office and went to find Fenton, his friend and 170 colleague. He found him by the coffee machine. Before he could ask him about Miller, Fenton spoke.

'Ah, Baker, you're back! What do you think of our new boss?'

'New boss?' What happened to Miller?' he asked. 175

'Miller? Don't you know? He's been promoted. Head Office gave him a sort of test – an imaginary case he had to solve. I think it gave him a bit of trouble, but he managed to find [2] the answer in the end.

Baker's mouth hung open. [3] 180

'Don't look so surprised,' Fenton continued. 'Miller's a very intelligent man.'

---

1. **place** : position.
2. **managed to find** : succeeded in finding.
3. **hung open** : (hang, hung, hung) expression made by face because of shock or surprise.

After reading

1 **Answer these questions.**

a. Why did Baker go to Miller's office?

....

b. Why did Cranberry go to the library?

....

c. What did he find in the book?

....

d. What took him to Madame Eve's?

....

e. How many times did he go to the cemetery?

....

f. When did Jenkins leave Cranberry?

....

2 **Read the sentences below and decide which refer to Cranberry (C), Jenkins (J), Madame Eve (E) and Baker (B).**

	C	J	E	B
a. It wasn't difficult at all.	☐	☐	☐	☐
b. I'll wait here, sir.	☐	☐	☐	☐
c. How much is it?	☐	☐	☐	☐
d. They're delivering the table tomorrow.	☐	☐	☐	☐
e. You've got a very beautiful house.	☐	☐	☐	☐
f. I'm sorry but she's very ill.	☐	☐	☐	☐
g. I can't find it anywhere.	☐	☐	☐	☐
h. I hid it in the bed.	☐	☐	☐	☐
i. Let's go skiing.	☐	☐	☐	☐
j. To the library, please.	☐	☐	☐	☐

3 Fill in the missing prepositions.

into	in	for	of	on	up	at

a. Cranberry is leaving .... Cortina tomorrow.

b. The library is .... the end .... this road.

c. Jenkins waited .... Cranberry in the car.

d. The book was .... the top shelf. The librarian climbed .... the step-ladder to get it.

e. Did Cranberry believe .... the supernatural? [1]

f. When Baker walked .... the room, Miller was waiting.

4 Match the words in column A with the correct synonyms in column B (refer to meaning in the story).

A	B
a. quiet	worried
b. clever	silent
c. ghost	curious
d. inquisitive	antique
e. anxious	damaged
f. very old	private
g. broken	spirit
h. position	convince
i. confidential	room
j. persuade	answer
k. space	fate
l. reply	intelligent
m. destiny	place

1. **the supernatural** : things which cannot be explained by science.

5 Match a sentence from column A with another sentence in column B. Then join the sentences by using the following words to make one sentence.

because	so	and	but

A	B
a. Miller asked Baker to solve the mystery.	He couldn't find the necklace.
b. Baker read the report.	He didn't go to the police.
c. Cranberry dug up his mother's grave.	His mother was very ill.
d. Jenkins left Cranberry.	He solved the mystery.
e. Cranberry had no proof.	He went on holiday.
f. Baker took some money out of the bank.	He didn't know why.
g. Cranberry wanted to go to the library.	He wanted promotion.

6 **A** Find words in the story that are the opposite of the following:

a. go out   ....

b. calm   ....

c. question (noun)   ....

d. finish   ....

e. modern   ....

f. close (verb)   ....

g. remember   ....

h. win   ....

i. full   ....

j. light   ....

k. well   ....

B **Now complete the following sentences by using some of the opposites from 6A.**

a. I've always liked old furniture, how much is that .... chair?

b. It's really hot in here, can you .... the window?

c. Matthew had to take antibiotics [1] when he was .... last month.

d. I'm not very lucky at playing cards, I always ....

e. Don't .... my birthday, it's tomorrow!

f. Don't stay outside in the rain, ... and get dry.

---

1. **antibiotics** : chemicals which can kill harmful bacteria in the body.

7 Fill in the blanks with the words below, and then number the
sentences in the right order. Some words can be used twice.

> handle   librarian   butler   receipt   pawnshop
> bought   library   grandmother's   address   visiting
> clairvoyant   past   luck   burying   mother's   night

☐ **a.** Cranberry woke up one morning and decided he wanted to go
to the ....
He asked James, his ...., to drive him there in the Rolls.

☐ **b.** Cranberry was amazed to discover that Madame Eve knew
everything about his ...., his childhood, his girlfriends
and his financial problems.

☐ **c.** When he arrived at the library, he went straight to the
.... and asked her for a copy of *Strange Destiny*.

☐ **d.** She also told him that his .... could be changed only
by .... his heirloom in his .... grave.

☐ **e.** The .... card had an .... in London that took
him to see Madame Eve, a ....

☐ **f.** When he opened the book a .... fell out of it. It was
from the local ....

☐ **g.** The .... of the mirror was loose and in it he found
a .... card.

☐ **h.** Cranberry went straight to the pawnbroker, gave in the
.... and .... a small, antique mirror.

☐ **i.** That .... Cranberry took his great .... diamond
necklace and buried it in the cemetery.

26

The Penfriend

Before reading

1 Fill in the following application form about yourself.

Name ....

Address ....

Nationality [1] ....

Age ....

School ....

How many languages do you speak? ....

Why are you studying English? ....

....

What do you like doing in your free time? ....

....

What kind of music do you like? ....

Have you ever had a penfriend? ....

From which country? ....

....

Give a brief description of whom you would like to

write to (age, sex, nationality etc.) ....

....

....

....

....

....

1. **nationality** : the official right to belong to a country.

2 One of the characters in the story is a teenager with problems. Can you put her problems in order of importance for YOU!

"I haven't got a girlfriend/boyfriend!"

1.

"I'm too fat!"

2.

"I can't go to discos!"

3.

"I've got too much homework!"

4.

"My parents don't understand me!"

5.

"I haven't got enough money!"

6.

"I hate school!"

7.

"I have to be home by 10 p.m."

8.

—   ORDER OF IMPORTANCE   +

Have you got any problems that aren't in the list? Write them in the space below.

....

....

....

....

The Penfriend

Trudy had argued with her parents again. She couldn't stand it [1] anymore. She was old enough to look after herself! Every time she wanted to go out it was the same old story. [2]

5 They questioned her about where she was going, and whom she was going out with. She felt that her parents didn't trust her at all. Things were getting worse and worse.

Tony had invited her to a party on Saturday night. When she told her parents about it, they said she could go but... she
10 had to be home by ten o'clock.

Her friends knew that her parents treated her like a child, and they often teased [3] her about it. Most of her friends had

---

1. **stand it** : tolerate the situation.
2. **the same old story** : the same questions again and again.
3. **teased** : made fun of.

ThE PenfrieNd

really liberal [1] parents and could do what they liked. She
sometimes thought about sharing a flat with her friend,
Sharon, but she knew it was only a dream. The money she   15
earned from babysitting [2] wasn't even enough to buy herself
some new clothes.

If she didn't go to the party with Tony, he'd probably never
ask her out again. That's what usually happened. She got a lot
of invitations but she always refused. It was much easier saying   20
no than explaining why she had to be home by ten o'clock.

Trudy turned the music up louder and threw herself onto
the bed. She thought she could hear her mother shouting at
her to turn the music down, but she didn't care. She had lots
of homework to do, but couldn't be bothered. [3] Instead, she   25
opened a magazine and started looking through it when
something caught her eye. [4]

'Are you depressed? [5] *Do you feel as though your life is not
your own? You're not alone. Please write to me. Susan'*

The address followed. Trudy was pleased to see she wasn't   30
the only one with problems. She found it difficult to talk to
her friends – they didn't understand her. Maybe this Susan
could give her some advice.

She sat up and reached for a pen and paper. It took her half
an hour to write a long letter. She wrote about her parents and   35

1. **liberal** : open-minded.
2. **babysitting** : looking after someone's child.
3. **couldn't be bothered** : didn't want to do it.
4. **caught her eye** : (catch, caught, caught) attracted her attention.
5. **depressed** : sad and hopeless.

ThE PenfrieNd

her problems in communicating with them, and also about how she felt trapped.[1]

When she had finished the letter she felt much better. She posted it the next day.

A week later, she got a reply. It was a long letter from Susan. As she read it Trudy realized that they both had many things in common,[2] apart from the fact that Susan had left school. The last paragraph made Trudy realize that Susan's problems were worse than hers.

> ... Things are getting unbearable.[3] They never speak to me, or ask my opinion about anything. I'm almost ignored. They don't really want me here. I heard them planning their holidays yesterday. They're thinking of going abroad and leaving me here on my own.[4] I don't know what to do...
> Write soon.
> Susan

Trudy felt sorry for her new friend. She wrote back the same day.

---

1. **trapped** : unable to escape from a situation.
2. **in common** : shared.
3. **unbearable** : intolerable.
4. **on my own** : alone.

55 Dear Susan,
Thanks for your letter, and for your advice. You were
right. It's much better trying to talk to my parents,
than shouting and slamming [1] doors! I'm going to the
party with Tony tonight but I have to be home by eleven.
60 It's not exactly what I wanted but it's better than
nothing. What about your problems? Couldn't you go on
holiday with them or speak to them? Tell them you don't
want to stay at home on your own.
By the way, [2] have you got a boyfriend?
65 Write soon and let me know.
Trudy

Things got better for Trudy. She learned how to explain
things to her parents and they began to understand that she
needed her freedom. At school she was doing well. She
70 studied hard and her results were always good.

While things got better for Trudy, they got worse for Susan.
The next letter made Trudy very sad.

---

1. **slamming** : shutting doors with a loud noise.
2. **by the way** : (used to introduce a new subject).

ThE PenfrieNd

Dear Trudy,

I'm happy to hear that you're now getting on with your parents. I wish I could say the same for myself. I mentioned going on holiday with them, but it was useless. They don't want me here — they want their freedom. After a terrible row,[1] they sent me to my room. They say if I want to live here, I have to do what they say.

I had a bad night — I'm so depressed. Nobody wants me. I haven't got a boyfriend — there was one but they frightened him away. I haven't seen or heard from him since. They're jealous! They don't even want me to write letters.

Please write soon.

Susan

Trudy wondered[2] what kind of parents the poor girl had. Trudy started writing a reply immediately.

---

1. **row** : noisy and sometimes violent disagreement.
2. **wondered** : asked herself.

90 Dear Susan,
   I got your letter this morning. You're in a difficult
   situation but don't forget that adults often say things
   they don't mean. I'm sure they don't realize how
   much they are hurting you. Tell them you're not a
95 child anymore – sending you to your room won't
   solve anything!
   I can understand them not wanting you to go out at
   night (just like my parents!) but writing a few letters...
   What harm can that do?
100 Things here are getting better. There's a concert next week
   and they say I can go. I think they're beginning to like Tony!
   Bye for now.
   Trudy

Susan's reply came after a few days.

105 Dear Trudy,

I'm pleased things are improving for you – the situation here is getting worse! They went out for the day yesterday and wanted me to stay at home on my own. When I told them I wanted to go out they locked me in my

110 room. I can't stand it anymore – I feel really depressed. You're the only person I confide in.[1] Now, they're refusing to post my letters so I give them to the boy who brings the newspapers. As for going out in the evenings, they won't even let me out during the day. I used to meet a

115 group of friends every Saturday but they stopped me going. Now I've lost contact with them all.

I know they wish I didn't exist, and sometimes, so do I.

Please write soon. Your letters are the only thing I look forward to.[2]

120 Susan

Trudy was shocked. Susan was being mentally tortured! She decided to show the letters to her parents.

'Oh, Trudy. You don't really believe everything that Susan writes, do you? It seems to me that she's got a very vivid

125 imagination,' her father said.

---

1. **the only person I confide in** : the only person I trust enough to tell a secret.
2. **look forward to** : wait for something with pleasure.

The Penfriend

'Write to her again,' her mother suggested. 'Invent something yourself. Play the same game.'

Trudy wasn't convinced.[1] She wrote back the next day.

> Dear Susan,
> Are you on the phone?[2] Why don't you call the police? 130
> What they're doing to you is a crime – they can't treat
> you like this!
> It's your life – you've got to change it now!
> Please let me know what you decide to do.
> Trudy 135

This time Susan took a while[3] to reply. The contents of the letter didn't surprise Trudy.

---

1. **convinced** : certain.
2. **Are you on the phone?** : Have you got a phone?
3. **a while** : a long time.

> Dear Trudy,
>
> Thanks for your advice – I appreciate [1] you're trying to help me.
> I almost made the phone call you suggested but the more I
> thought about it, the more I decided against it. I know you
> find it hard to understand, but even though they treat me so
> badly, I still love them. If I call the police, or social services, [2]
> it'll create even more problems. Then, the police will arrest
> them. I'm not sure this is what I want. They're not too bad if
> I obey them...
> Please write soon.
> Susan

140

145

Trudy began to think that her parents were right. If Susan

150 was really desperate, she would ask for help. She wrote back
but didn't mention Susan's problems. Instead, she wrote about
herself and Tony, and about life in general. This time she
enclosed a photograph, and asked for one in exchange.

When Trudy received Susan's reply, she knew she had to

155 do something.

---

1. **appreciate** : recognise or understand.
2. **social services** : service provided by the government to help people with problems.

ThE PenfrieNd

Dear Trudy,

Thanks for your photo. You sounded [1] really happy in your
letter. Things are a bit different here.

A few days ago I wanted to go out for a walk, but they wouldn't
let me. I was so annoyed. [2] I told them I was   160
going to call the police. I've never seen them so angry,
especially her. She slapped [3] me, and told me to go up to
my room. As I was going up the stairs I slipped [4] and fell.
I was a bit bruised, [5] but luckily didn't break any bones. I had
to stay in bed for a day, but I'm much better now.   165
I'm sure they didn't mean to do it - but since then we
haven't spoken. Maybe it's better, at least we don't argue!
Hope to hear from you soon.

Susan

Trudy took the letter to her parents and insisted on   170
phoning the police. Her mother had an idea. Her friend Maggie
was a social worker. [6] She phoned her and explained the
situation. Half an hour later, Maggie called at their house.

1. **sounded** : seemed.
2. **annoyed** : angry.
3. **slapped** : hit across the face.
4. **slipped** : lost her balance.
5. **was a bit bruised** : got some dark marks on the body caused by the fall.
6. **social worker** : (job) person who helps people with problems.

The Penfriend

She wanted to read the letters. When she'd seen them, she told Trudy that she had done well to call her. Maggie explained that a social worker would go and see Susan. She promised to keep Trudy informed.[1]

Trudy didn't write back to Susan. She preferred to wait and hear from Maggie. Besides, she didn't know if Susan wanted to write to her again, after what she had done.

One evening, Maggie came to visit them bringing them news of Susan. It seemed that Susan had suffered [2] physically [3] as well as mentally.[4] At first, Susan would not admit that she had been treated badly. When she saw the letters she had sent Trudy, she agreed to tell the truth. After a brief stay in hospital, the social worker found her somewhere to live. She had given a letter to Maggie, for Trudy.

> Dear Trudy,
>
> At first I was upset [5] when I found out that you'd contacted the social services. Now I understand why you did it. I'm very happy here; the people I live with are very friendly and kind.
>
> I live quite near to you now – why don't you come and see me? Hope to see you soon.
>
> Susan

1. **keep Trudy informed** : let Trudy have a lot of information about Susan.
2. **suffered** : felt pain.
3. **physically** : related to the body.
4. **mentally** : related to the mind.
5. **upset** : unhappy.

A few days later, she took the train down to Hampton and then took a taxi to the address on the letter. A young girl answered the door. 'Susan's in the living room. She's waiting for you ...' When Trudy walked into the room, she thought

200 there had been a mistake. An old woman was sitting in an armchair reading a book. Trudy turned to leave, but the woman called her.

'You're Trudy, aren't you? I'm Susan,' she said, putting down her book.

205 'Susan?' Trudy answered perplexed.[1] 'I thought...'

'Yes, I know. You thought you were writing to a young girl who had problems with her parents. Now you've discovered I'm an old woman who had problems with her son and wife.'

'Why didn't you tell me?' she asked.

210 'Because you didn't ask me,' Susan replied, laughing. 'I didn't lie to you, I just didn't mention a few details.'

'Yes, but why?'

'If you had known I was old enough to be your grandmother, would you have written to me?' Susan asked.

215 'I suppose not!' Trudy admitted.

'I enjoyed your letters so much. Young people are so full of life but think they're the only ones with problems... God only knows how many people there are in my situation. I was forced to live with a son who only wanted me for my pension.[2]

220 After all I've done for him!'

---

1. **perplexed** : showing worry and confusion.
2. **pension** : a sum of money paid regularly by the government.

ThE PenfrieNd

Susan and Trudy talked for a while. It was as though they had known each other for years.

As Trudy left the house she could see Susan in the garden chatting [1] away happily to her new friends. She decided to write to her the next day.

---

1. **chatting** : talking in a friendly manner.

After reading

1 Are these sentences true (T) or false (F)?

	T	F
a. Trudy started to write to a penfriend because she was depressed.	☐	☐
b. Susan didn't reply to the letter for a month.	☐	☐
c. Trudy is going to a concert next week.	☐	☐
d. Trudy wasn't doing very well at school.	☐	☐
e. Susan hasn't got a boyfriend.	☐	☐
f. Trudy received two photographs from her penfriend.	☐	☐
g. Susan didn't call the police.	☐	☐
h. When Susan saw the social worker she told the truth.	☐	☐
i. Susan had problems with her mother and father.	☐	☐
j. Trudy still writes to Susan.	☐	☐

Now correct the false sentences.

2 Underline the correct words.

"Susan's life sounded *great / awful*! When I received her last letter I was really *pleased / worried*. I wanted to call the *police / social worker* but my *mother / sister* stopped me. Instead I phoned a friend of my *mother's / father's* who came round straight away when she *heard / read* about the problem. I showed her the *photos / letters* and gave her Susan's *address / phone number*. I think somebody went round there the next *day / month*. Susan's *father / son* wasn't very happy when he saw her..."

3 Complete these sentences with the correct forms of the verbs.

    a. If Trudy .... (*go*) to the party, she'll have a good time.

    b. If I .... (*call*) the police, they'll contact the social services.

    c. The police will arrest them, if Trudy .... (*tell*) them about Susan.

    d. If you .... (*write*) to a British penfriend, you'll improve your English.

    e. If Trudy .... (*not/go*) to the party, Tony won't ask her again.

4 Here is a letter written by Susan to Trudy. Can you complete the gaps with the correct positive or negative forms of the verbs (Present Perfect or Past Simple)?

take   go   change   visit   live   write   be   catch   improve

Dear Trudy,

How are you? I'm sorry I .... to you for such a long time but I .... so busy since you .... me. By the way, thanks for the chocolates! My life .... completely - I .... here for two months now and I'm doing so many new things. I've started studying French and also doing some travelling. I .... to Paris last week for a couple of days - it was very exciting! We .... the ferry from Dover to Calais and then .... the train to Paris. I hope my French ....!

That's all for now. Please come and visit me if you have time.

Lots of love.

Susan

5 Look at these advertisements from the International Penfriends Association. Choose one of them and write a letter telling them about yourself, your interests, your dislikes etc.

British student, 18, wants to write in English to anybody in the world! Likes: Rock Concerts, travelling, Italian food. Dislikes: studying, discos and politics. Please write to:- Robert Walsh, 16 Whelan Drive, Cardiff

Australian unemployed [1] teenager, 18, wants to write to students of English all over the world. Likes: swimming, surfing, reading, cooking, music and Italian girls! Dislikes: cars, noise, money. Write to:- Pete Salsa, 252 Spring Avenue, Sydney

American teenager, 16, from Texas, wants a penfriend in Europe (preferably male!)
Likes: Oasis,[2] buying clothes, eating.
Dislikes: All sports!
Write to:- Kerry Lovack, P.O. Box 1642, Texas

1. **unemployed** : not having a paid-job.
2. **oasis** : a place in a desert where there are trees and water.

6 **Look at these sentences:**

Trudy <u>has to</u> be home by 10 o'clock in the evening.

I <u>have to</u> stay in my room when my son goes out.

Can you complete the following sentences using the above structure?

a. I have to ....

b. My mother has to ....

c. Teachers ....

d. I don't ....

e. A politician ....

f. I ....

g. Students ....

7 **Do your parents understand you? Try the following quiz.**

a. What would your parents say if you wanted to go to a disco?

☐ Yes, if you come home early.

☐ No, you're too young.

☐ Yes, if we can come too!

b. If you wanted to go on holiday with your boyfriend/girlfriend, your parents would

☐ give you the money for the tickets.

☐ go with you.

☐ lock you in your room!

c. If you wanted a part-time job after school what job would your parents suggest?

☐ Babysitting.

☐ Working in a shop.

☐ Cleaning your bedroom!

d. How would your parents react if you wanted to go and share a flat with a friend?

☐ Buy you a flat and help you choose the furniture.

☐ Think you were mad.

☐ Stop you in some way!

e. What would you do if your parents decided to travel around the world and leave you at home?

If ....

I would ....

....

....

....

8 **Complete the following sentences:**

a. If I won a lot of money, I would ....

b. If I failed my exams, I would ....

c. If I were older, I ....

d. If my parents stopped me going to discos, I ....

e. If I left school, I ....

9 **Do you think old people are treated well in your country?**
Do you think old people should live with their families or be put into homes? Write a few sentences to express your opinion.

....

....

....

....

The Big Mistake

Before reading

1 **What kind of holiday do you like?**

a. Which do you prefer?
- [ ] The sea.
- [ ] The mountains.
- [ ] Cities.

b. What do you like doing?
- [ ] Going to discos.
- [ ] Reading books.
- [ ] Eating.
- [ ] Going sightseeing.

c. With whom do you go on holiday?
- [ ] With my friends.
- [ ] With my family.
- [ ] On my own.

d. How long do you go on holiday for?
- [ ] Less than a week.
- [ ] More than a week.
- [ ] More than a month.

e. How do you feel when you return?
- [ ] Happy and relaxed.
- [ ] Depressed.
- [ ] No difference.

2 **A** Match the definitions in column A with the crimes in column B.

Column A	Column B
a. Burglary	to enter a house with the intention of stealing
b. Murder	to steal from a bank
c. Theft	to take goods from a shop without paying
d. Robbery	to kill illegally
e. Shoplifting	to take away a person and ask for money in return
f. Kidnapping	to steal

B Use your dictionary to find the names of the people who commit [1] these crimes. One is done for you.

Example: *burglary / **burglar***

....

....

....

....

....

1. **commit** : do something illegal.

53

ThE Big MIstaKe

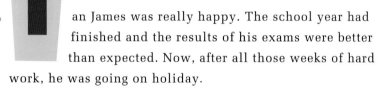

an James was really happy. The school year had
finished and the results of his exams were better
than expected. Now, after all those weeks of hard
work, he was going on holiday.

5 Fortunately, his rich uncle, Uncle Patrick, hadn't forgotten his
promise. Ian had spoken to him on the phone two nights
before – everything was planned. Uncle Patrick had left for
France so his house by the sea was empty. He'd left the fridge [1]
full of food and drink and the key was under the doormat. [2]

10 Ian could use the house until his uncle returned. Paula, his
girlfriend was coming to stay with him the next day and they
would be able to spend some time together.

He stared through the train window watching the houses,
fields and people go by. The train began to slow down as it

---

1. **fridge** : refrigerator.　　　　2. **doormat** :

The Big Mistake

came into Bridgeview Station.

The fat woman that sat opposite him was still asleep. The train stopped suddenly.

'Ooh,' she exclaimed, standing up and putting her head out of the window. 'It's Bridgeview.' She picked up her handbag and rushed to the door. 'It's lucky I woke up, otherwise I would have gone on to Littlepoint!'

So Ian knew he had to get off the train at the next station. He looked at his watch as the train left the station. Almost six o'clock. He was hungry and started thinking about all the food in the fridge that was waiting for him.

The scenery changed. In the distance he could see the sea and a few people on the beach. Ian had never been to his uncle's house before. He hadn't realized that he lived so close to the sea – he hoped it wasn't too polluted. [1]

He could smell the salty air of the sea.

The train hooted [2] as it approached the station of Littlepoint. Ian grabbed [3] his suitcase and got off the train. Luckily, there was a taxi free. He put his case in the boot [4] and asked the driver to take him to Cliffview.

'What number?' the driver asked.

'Twenty eight,' Ian replied.

---

1. **polluted** : not clean.
2. **hooted** : made a short loud high sound.
3. **grabbed** : took suddenly.
4. **boot** : (here) a covered space at the back of a car.

The Big Mistake

It didn't take long to get there. The taxi stopped outside the largest house in the street.

Ian paid the taxi driver and picked up his case. As he walked up the path, he wondered who had planted all the flowers in the garden. He didn't think his uncle was the type to be interested in gardening. He continued up the path, and stopped at the door. He lifted up the doormat. The key was exactly where his Uncle Patrick had promised.

He opened the door and entered the hall, [1] closing the door behind him. He left his suitcase by the stairs, walked through the hallway and into the lounge. [2]

There were two long sofas in one corner of the room and a table and chairs occupied the centre. The floor was covered by a thick brown carpet and beige [3] curtains hung at the windows. There was an enormous cabinet containing a lot of different ornaments, [4] and a vase of flowers on the table.

Ian explored [5] the rest of the ground floor. There was a bathroom, a dining room, a small study and a large kitchen.

Ian carried his suitcase upstairs. There were three bedrooms and a bathroom. He chose the biggest room and threw his case on the bed. He was too tired to unpack it. He went into the bathroom and had a quick shower. He left the towels on the floor and went to get dressed. He emptied his case, throwing his clothes on the chair. He would hang them

1.   **hall** : the room in a house into which the front door opens.
2.   **lounge** : living room.
3.   **beige** : very light yellowish brown.
4.   **ornaments** : decorations.
5.   **explored** : examined.

up in the wardrobe [1] later. Now he was hungry so he went downstairs to get some food. He opened the fridge – what a disappointment! There were two boiled potatoes, some ham and a bottle of milk. It wasn't much, but Ian had no choice. He
65 ate his meal in the lounge, in front of the television.

When he had finished he took the dishes into the kitchen and threw them into the sink. [2] He heard the plate break. When he returned to the lounge, his favourite quiz show was starting. He lay down on the sofa to watch television.

70 After a while, his eyes felt heavy. He was tired. He turned off the television and went upstairs to bed.

He had been asleep for about an hour, when he was awoken by a loud noise. A window being smashed! [3] He heard the glass fall to the floor. He sat up in bed and switched on the bedside
75 lamp. He could hear voices from downstairs. Burglars!

He sat still for a moment, wondering what to do. The telephone was downstairs so he couldn't call for help. Should he go downstairs and face them? No... They may be dangerous.

He heard them walking through the hallway, and turning
80 on a light switch. Ian got out of bed and crept [4] onto the landing. [5]

He could hear the thieves talking – he listened to what they were saying.

1. **wardrobe** : a large cupboard that you hang clothes in.
2. **sink** : basin in the kitchen used for washing up.
3. **smashed** : broken noisily into small pieces.
4. **crept** : (creep, crept, crept) moved slowly and quietly.
5. **landing** : area at the top of the stairs.

The Big Mistake

'Where did you bury [1] him?'

'I think it's better if you don't know. Don't worry, nobody   85
will ever find him.'

'Oh God, I didn't mean to do it!'

Ian trembled.[2] The thieves had killed someone and buried
the body.

He looked down the stairs and saw the two men. One of   90
them was sitting on the sofa, the other stood leaning against
the table.[3] Both were wearing black suits. The man near the
table had a red stain on his white shirt. Blood!?

Ian walked as quietly as possible into the bedroom. He
closed the door behind him. How could he escape?   95

He thought of a film that he had once seen. A man had
escaped from a burning house by using the bed sheets as a
rope. Ian ran to the window. He looked down. It was a long
drop.[4] There was no grass beneath him, just concrete.[5]

Suddenly the voices were nearer. They were coming up the   100
stairs. Ian shook with fear. He didn't know where to hide. He
looked around the room desperately. The wardrobe! He ran to
it, climbed inside, and pulled the door shut.

The voices and footsteps approached. Someone opened the
bedroom door – Ian stopped breathing. One of the men spoke.   105

---

1. **bury** : put under ground.
2. **trembled** : shook slightly.
3. **stood leaning against the table** : stood with part of the body touching the table as
   a support.
4. **long drop** : long way to the ground.
5. **concrete** : building material made by mixing cement with sand, gravel and water.

'I told you. There's nobody here. Look for yourself.'

They closed the door and continued along the landing.

Ian jumped out of the wardrobe and ran to the door – he opened it slowly. He checked that the landing was empty. The
110   voices were coming from one of the larger bedrooms – they were looking for money!

Ian ran quickly out of the room and down the stairs – he had to call the police! He picked up the telephone and dialled 999. The phone was dead. [1] The murderers had cut the outside
115   wires.

How could he call for help? He looked down at his bare feet. [2] His slippers [3] were upstairs. So were his clothes. He couldn't go out into the cold night in his pyjamas![4]

The light on the landing suddenly came on. He could hear
120   someone coming down the stairs. Ian threw himself onto the floor, behind the table. One of the men had gone into the kitchen. He heard him opening a cupboard, and pouring out a glass of water.

He had an idea. Now that the men had separated, maybe he
125   could face them on his own. He moved as quietly as possible and hid behind the kitchen door. The man finished his drink and walked towards the hall. Ian was ready. Just as the man put his foot in the doorway, Ian pushed the door as hard as he

---

1.   **The phone was dead** : The phone wasn't working.
2.   **bare feet** : he had nothing on his feet.
3.   **slippers** :
4.   **pyjamas** : clothes worn in bed.

could. The man shouted with pain and fell onto the floor. Ian
130   quickly closed the door and turned the key.

He knew that the man's cries would soon be heard by his
accomplice [1] so he had to try and stop the other one. He didn't
have time to think. The man was coming down the stairs.

Ian crouched [2] down behind a cupboard. It was dark and he
135   couldn't be seen. The man lost his balance and fell down the
last few steps. Ian unplugged [3] the telephone and ran quickly
to where the man lay. He was face down and not fully
conscious.[4] Using the telephone wire, Ian tied the man's hands
behind his back.

140   'Who are you? What do you want?' the man cried.

Ian didn't answer, and ran up the stairs to his bedroom. He
found his slippers and his dressing gown. [5] Now he had to run
and get help.

He jumped over the man at the bottom of the stairs,
145   ignoring his cries, and ran towards the front door. He threw it
open and screamed with fright!

There before him was the man that he'd locked in the
kitchen! Blood was dripping from his nose. The man took hold
of Ian's arms and put them behind his back – he was very
150   strong. Ian couldn't escape!

1. **accomplice** : person who helps another to do something illegal.

2. **crouched** : made himself smaller by bending his knees.

3. **unplugged** : disconnected.

4. **conscious** : awake.

5. **dressing gown :**

ThE Big MistaKe

'You little hooligan! [1] You forgot about the back door in the kitchen, didn't you?'

He pushed Ian onto the sofa.

'Bill, untie me!'

The man that Ian had left at the bottom of the stairs stood up and walked towards them. The telephone hung from the wire behind his back.

'Who's this?' he asked.

'I don't know, but I'm going to teach him a lesson!'

He put his hand to the inside pocket of his jacket. He was looking for his gun!

'Damn, I must have left it in the car,' the man said. He went out of the front door.

Ian shook with fear. He looked around him. He had no chance of escaping. The men were too big and too strong. Maybe he could convince them to let him go.

'Listen,' he said, 'I've got some money upstairs in my case. You can have it if you let me go. I won't tell anyone!'

'What?' the man laughed. 'You're joking!' [2]

The other man came back in. He was holding a small black object. Ian closed his eyes. It was the end.

'No, no!' he begged. [3]

'Sorry. You deserve it,' came the reply.

Ian waited, his eyes still closed tightly.

---

1. **hooligan** : a disorderly young person who behaves violently and cause damage.
2. **joking** : not serious.
3. **begged** : asked anxiously.

175 'Hello, police? I've just found a thief in my house. Yes, he's here in front of me.'

Ian opened his eyes in amazement. [1] The little black object was a telephone!

'Your house?' he cried. They didn't answer him.

180 'The address? Twenty eight, Cliffview. Yes, he's under control. We'll wait.'

'What do you mean, your house? This is my uncle's house!'

'Try telling that to the police!'

Ian tried to convince them that he was telling the truth.

185 They wouldn't listen.

A few minutes later, a police car arrived. Ian was arrested.

At the police station he was questioned but nobody would believe him.

He was allowed to phone his uncle.

190 'Talk to them, Uncle Patrick. Tell them that the house is yours!'

His uncle's reply shocked him.

'I can't!' Uncle Patrick replied. 'It isn't my house. Mine is number twenty six!'

195 Uncle Patrick spoke to the police and explained the situation. Ian had made a terrible mistake!

'What about the man they buried? I heard them talking about the murder!' he said to the policeman.

The two men looked at each other.

200 'What man?' the policeman asked.

---

1. **amazement** : surprise.

ThE Big MistaKe

'That wasn't a man! It was a dog. We hit it with the car
coming back from the restaurant. It didn't have a collar, it was
a stray. [1] What else could I do?'

'And the blood on your shirt?'

'That's not blood!' the policeman replied. 'It's wine. I can
smell it from here.' 205

Ian felt stupid. He had to stay in the station while the
police and one of the men went to check that nothing had
been stolen. When they returned, they had Ian's suitcase with
them. It was almost eight o'clock in the morning. Ian was not 210
charged, and was free to go. He apologized [2] to the two men,
and was accompanied to his uncle's house. [3] This time, the
right one!

Ian was left in the doorway of twenty six, Cliffview. He'd
had a bad night, and he was tired. He found the door key 215
under the mat. There was a letter under the door. He bent to
pick it up. It was from Paula. It read:

> After three hours on the train, I expected to find you at home.
> Don't bother phoning [4] — I don't want to speak to you!

Ian had some explaining to do. 220

---

1. **stray** : animal without a home.
2. **apologized** : said sorry.
3. **and was accompanied to his uncle's house** : went to his uncle's house with
   someone.
4. **Don't bother phoning** : Don't worry about phoning.

After reading

1 Put these pictures into the order as they appear in the story. Then match the following actions with the pictures.

    a. arrive at the house

    b. watch TV

    c. have a shower

    d. go upstairs

    e. go to bed

    f. hear a noise

    g. tie the man's hands

    h. be arrested

☐ ☐

☐ ☐

2 Put the sentences in Activity 1 into the past tense to write a summary of the story. Add other details to make the story more complete.

Example:
Ian arrived at the house at 7 o'clock.

Use the following words to help you.

> bedroom TV and but because
> tired landing police downstairs

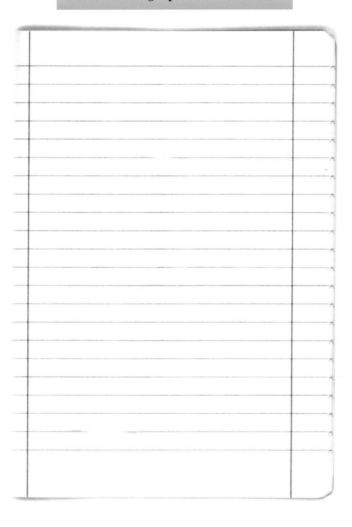

3 **Do this quiz without looking at the story!**

a. Ian is going on holiday to
   - ☐ Bigpoint.
   - ☐ Littlepoint.
   - ☐ Smallpoint.

b. What does Ian eat?
   - ☐ Potatoes.
   - ☐ Chicken.
   - ☐ Rice.

c. The key was
   - ☐ in the door.
   - ☐ under the doormat.
   - ☐ in a flowerpot.

d. Ian watched
   - ☐ a soap opera.
   - ☐ a quiz show.
   - ☐ a documentary.

e. What did Ian forget in his room?
   - ☐ His slippers.
   - ☐ His book.
   - ☐ His pyjamas.

f. Ian dialled
   - ☐ 999.
   - ☐ 666.
   - ☐ 333.

g. Ian locked the thief in the
   - ☐ kitchen.
   - ☐ bathroom.
   - ☐ toilet.

h. Uncle Patrick's house is at number

☐ 26.

☐ 27.

☐ 28.

i. What did the man have in his pocket?

☐ A knife.

☐ A gun.

☐ A mobile phone.

j. Ian offered the thieves

☐ some money.

☐ some tea.

☐ a gun.

k. The stray dog was

☐ in the road.

☐ in the field.

☐ in the house.

l. The stain on the man's shirt was

☐ blood.

☐ wine.

☐ tomato ketchup.

Now check your answers in the story.

4 Complete the puzzle.

1. Someone who steals.
2. An object which keeps things cold.
3. The top of a staircase.
4. Another name for 'living room'.
5. Clothes you usually wear in bed.
6. What you feel when somebody kicks you hard.
7. A place where you catch a train.
8. The telephone is connected to this.
9. Something you need to buy things.
10. Something you put flowers in.

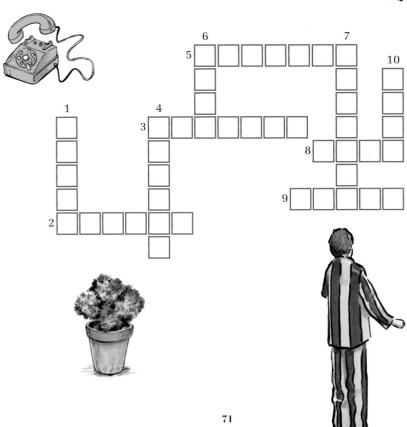

5 Complete the sentences with question tags.

Example: *You forgot about the kitchen door,* ***didn't you?***

a. The fridge is nearly empty, ...?

b. Ian got off the train at Littlepoint, ...?

c. He didn't eat much, ...?

d. Ian likes watching quiz shows, ...?

e. You're joking, ...?

f. The two men weren't thieves, ...?

g. That isn't blood, ...?

6 Can you correct the mistakes in the following sentences?

a. Ian came with the train yesterday.

   ....

b. Ian has arrived at Cliffview at about 6 o'clock.

   ....

c. Ian ate two boiled potato, a ham and drank a milk.

   ....

d. Ian tied the hands of the man.

   ....

e. The two men turned up the light.

   ....

f. Ian chose the most big room.

   ....

g. The thieves cutted the outside wires.

   ....

7 Underline the correct prepositions.

a. Turn (in, up, off) the light before you go to bed.

b. Ian got (on, in, off) the train at Littlepoint.

c. The train slowed (up, down, up) just before the station.

d. The thief looked (for, at, in) the gun in his pocket.

e. Ian picked (up, off, out) his clothes and put them in the wardrobe.

f. It was so dark, he turned (off, on, out) the light.

8 A Complete the spidergraph below.

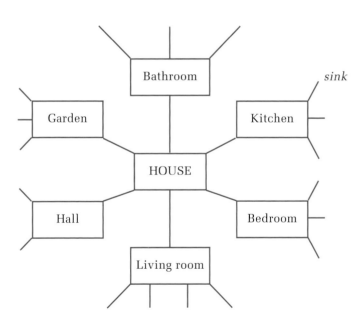

B Now complete these sentences.

a. You usually cook in the ....

b. Why don't you cut the .... in the garden?

c. I love watching .... in bed.

d. The .... in the bedroom is full of clothes.

e. British people usually hang up their coats in the

....

f. My mother used to wash clothes by hand, I prefer using a

..........................!

9 **Match the verbs in column A with the words in column B.**

A	B
a. You make	a train
b. You catch	television
c. You pick up	a shower
d. You look at	a mistake
e. You watch	clothes
f. You have	a suitcase
g. You hang up	the light
h. You switch on	a watch

10 **Can you think of another ending to the story? Write a few lines below.**

....

....

....

Listening

1 **Listen to the first part of the story (ll. 1-65) and correct the mistakes, if necessary.**

a. Ian had passed his exams.

....

b. Ian was going on holiday to the mountains.

....

c. His girlfriend Paula was arriving the next day.

....

d. Ian got off the train at Bridgeview.

....

e. He waited for a bus outside the station.

....

f. The ground floor had five rooms.

....

g. Ian went upstairs, took his clothes off and had a bath.

....

h. There wasn't much food in the fridge.

....

i. Ian ate his meal in the kitchen, in front of the television.

....

Now check your answers in the text.

2 While listening to the story tick (✓) the objects which are NOT mentioned.

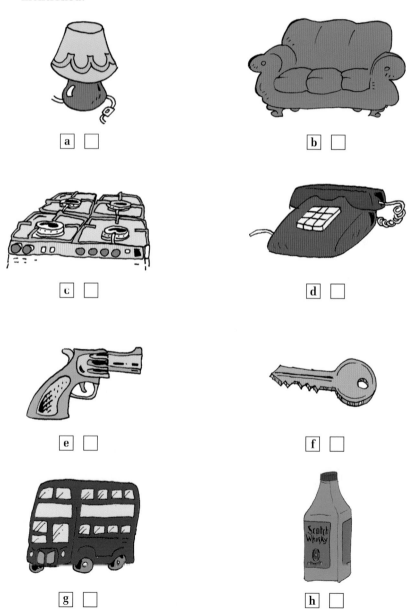

a ☐

b ☐

c ☐

d ☐

e ☐

f ☐

g ☐

h ☐

Marge aNd OLiVe

Before reading

1 **What do you do at home?**

	always	often	never
• do the shopping	☐	☐	☐
• do the washing up	☐	☐	☐
• do the cleaning	☐	☐	☐
• do the cooking	☐	☐	☐
• do the ironing	☐	☐	☐
• make the beds	☐	☐	☐
• put the rubbish out	☐	☐	☐
• lay the table	☐	☐	☐

What do you like doing the most? ....

What do you like doing the least? ....

2 **Underline the word that is different. Why is it different?**

a. beef	lamb	cow	chicken	pork
b. eggs	yoghurt	milk	coffee	cream
c. pasta	flour	rice	bread	beans
d. tea	milk	cornflakes	juice	coca-cola
e. apple	pineapple	grapes	pepper	melon
f. potato	cucumber	tomato	lettuce	cherry

3 **What do you think this story is about? Read the beginning of the story (ll. 1-10) to help you.**

• crime   • love   • horror   • adventure   • war

Now read the story to check your answers.

Marge  and Olive

 arge and Olive were two sisters who had lived together all their lives. They were both over seventy. When their father died leaving them the house and some money, it was Olive who was the boss. She was a little older than Marge and had a very bad temper. Marge was afraid of her, and soon learnt to do everything she was told to do. Olive did the shopping, paid the electricity, gas and water bills, and decided how to spend their money. Marge did the cleaning, the cooking and decided when to put the rubbish out to be collected.

Marge hadn't been shopping for a long time; she couldn't walk far because of her arthritis.[1] Besides, it wasn't necessary for her to go shopping – Olive was happy to go on her own.

5

10

---

1. **arthritis** : a state in which the joints of a person becomes painful, swollen and stiff.

The Big Mistake and Other Stories

Marge hated shopping days. Olive arrived home carrying
15 the heavy bags – always in a terrible mood ¹ – and ordered
Marge to make her a cup of tea. Then Marge would go and get
Olive's slippers. ² Olive would then start complaining and say
that Marge was lucky to have someone to do the shopping for
her. Marge nodded ³ silently. She knew it was better not to
20 argue with Olive. As Marge unpacked the shopping, putting
everything in the cupboards, Olive talked about the price of
things. Especially clothes. They were so expensive! That is
why they had to share them, or more exactly, Marge would
have Olive's old clothes.

25 Marge often asked her sister to buy her certain foods she
liked. Olive would always refuse, because she couldn't eat
these things herself. Cheese, milk and yoghurt would give her
terrible stomach pains. So Marge was left without.

Marge had a really difficult time when Olive was ill. She
30 would often have to get out of bed, late at night, to give Olive
a tablet for her angina. ⁴ Sometimes, Olive would wake her up
just because she wanted a cup of tea. Marge would always
obey. She didn't have the courage to refuse, and by now, she
was used to being treated badly.⁵ Besides, she had a secret
35 that helped her to put up with ⁶ Olive. Alfred was back!

---

1. **mood** : state of mind.
2. **slippers** :
3. **nodded** : moved her head up and down to show agreement.
4. **angina** : illness of the heart.
5. **she was used to being treated badly** : she learnt to accept being treated badly.
6. **put up with** : tolerate.

When Marge was much younger, Alfred had been her boyfriend, and they had planned to get married. Olive was really jealous and had done everything possible to separate the two. When she discovered that Alfred had been accused of
40 being a deserter [1] during the Second World War, she had told her father. Alfred had tried to explain that it had all been a mistake, but their father would not listen. He sent Alfred away, and ordered Marge not to see him again. Alfred left the town and later Marge heard that he had married someone else.
45 It took her a long time to forget him. She hated Olive for this and would never forgive her. [2]

Now, after all these years, Alfred had moved back into town. He had lost his wife a few years before, and had written to Marge asking her to forgive him. He was aware of the
50 terrible life that Marge had with her domineering [3] sister, and he felt responsible. In his first letter he told Marge how he wished that he had had the courage to explain to her father, instead of leaving her. He had been a coward. [4]

Marge was so pleased to receive his letter, that she forgave
55 him instantly. She wrote back and they began to write regularly. When Olive found out that Alfred had returned she tried to stop Marge writing to him. Marge ignored her and even managed to meet Alfred on the days when Olive went

1. **deserter** : person who leaves military service without permission.
2. **never forgive her** : never forget what Marge had done.
3. **domineering** : tending to control other people and ignoring their feelings.
4. **coward** : person who is afraid to face things.

shopping. They discovered that, despite their age, [1] and the
years that had passed, there was still something special   60
between them. Marge knew that if Olive discovered their
meetings, she would never see Alfred again. The thought of
this was terrible. Since Alfred had returned she had begun to
live again. They talked about lost friends, the dance halls that
they had danced in, and the wonderful music of the old days.   65
Sometimes they would sing together. Alfred would often bring
her chocolates, sweets and even the cream and yoghurt she
adored. [2] For the first time after so many years, Marge felt
wanted. It was the only thing that helped her through the day,
and she wasn't prepared to lose Alfred again.   70

Even though they met occasionally, [3] they decided that it
was better to keep writing to each other. Olive would be
suspicious if Marge stopped receiving letters. She'd miss
them, too. Olive would always read Marge's letters. She would
say she had a headache, and that she would go upstairs to lie   75
down. [4] But Marge knew it was just an excuse. [5] She had tried
hiding them but it was no use. Olive still found them.

At their last meeting, Alfred had asked her to marry him.
She had accepted, but what about Olive? Marge had thought
about leaving home, but this meant that she'd lose all her   80

---

1. **despite their age** : even though they were old.
2. **adored** : loved.
3. **occasionally** : not regularly.
4. **lie down** : have a rest on the bed.
5. **excuse** : a false reason.

money. Olive kept the bank books in her name. No, it was Olive that would have to go!

The next evening, Marge and Alfred met at the same time, at the same place. They talked about Olive and Alfred told
85 Marge about a plan that would finally solve everything. Marge listened carefully. Alfred was a genius! [1] She was sure that the plan would work, and soon they would be free. Alfred gave her a small tin and a letter. He told her to be very careful, and to make sure that Olive did not find them. Marge hid them in
90 her handbag. She could not wait, so they decided to carry out the plan the very next day.

Marge slept well that night. When Olive came downstairs for breakfast, she sang cheerfully to herself. Olive told her to shut up immediately, and complained that her tea was cold.
95 'The postman has already been,' Marge said, as she fried the eggs.

'So what?' Olive answered.

'There was just one letter – for me,' Marge replied.

Olive smiled. Good, she thought. Something for her to read
100 later on. Marge put the fried egg on Olive's plate.

'What shall we have for lunch today?' Marge asked.

'This egg is overcooked. [2] Give me the other one!' Olive ordered.

Marge obeyed, and said once again, 'What shall we ...'

---

1. **genius** : a very clever person.
2. **overcooked** : cooked for too long.

MARGE AND OLIVE

'I heard you the first time. I'm not deaf!' [1]

Marge jumped. She always did when Olive shouted.

'Meatloaf!' Olive continued. 'We always have meatloaf on Tuesday. And don't ask stupid questions!'

Marge nodded. They carried on eating their breakfast in silence.

Afterwards, Olive went into the garden to read the newspaper. Marge did her housework, then began to prepare the meatloaf. When she'd mixed the ingredients [2] together, she went to her handbag and found the small tin. She opened it and added the contents to the mixture. She mixed it in quickly, and hid the empty tin in the washing machine. Then she put the meatloaf in the oven to cook, and tried not to act suspiciously.

When the meatloaf was cooked, Marge sniffed [3] at it. She could not smell anything unusual. She was not hungry though. She told Olive that she had a headache, and that she did not want to eat. Olive was not particularly worried and started eating. Marge watched her from behind the kitchen door. That day, Olive ate more than usual.

After lunch, Marge did the washing up and Olive went to her room to lie down. Marge knew that she would read the letter. Things were going exactly as planned.

Olive rushed into Marge's room, found the letter, then returned to her own room to read it.

1. **deaf** : unable to hear.
2. **ingredients** : materials for preparing dishes.
3. **sniffed** : smelled.

130   Dear Marge,

The small tin that you found at the bottom of your garden is a

very strong poison that I bought for the mice in my cellar. [1]

You were right, my dear, it's the only way to get rid of [2] Olive.

Put it in the meatloaf that you mentioned.

135   She won't notice the taste or smell! The effect is almost

immediate. [3]

Please be patient,

All my love

Alfred

140   Olive read the letter quickly, then she read it again,
stopping at the word – poison. She threw the letter down, and
suddenly felt hot. An unbearable [4] pain began in her stomach,
and she cried out.

'Oh, my God! I've been poisoned. Help!'

145   Marge heard her from downstairs. She turned the volume of
the radio up and ignored her.

The pain got worse and Olive fell to the floor, trying to
breathe. How long would it take? Was she dying? Yes, the
letter had said that the poison was very strong! She lay on the

150   carpet waiting for someone to help her. She felt another pain,
much stronger than the other, in her chest. [5] Her left arm

---

1. **cellar** : room underground used for storing wine etc.
2. **get rid of** : become free of.
3. **immediate** : at once.
4. **unbearable** : too painful to bear.
5. **chest** : top front part of the body.

ached. It was her heart. She was having an attack. Where were her tablets? She called for Marge.

Marge sang to herself and waited. After a while, she could no longer hear Olive calling for her. She picked up the telephone and called for an ambulance. 155

When it arrived, Olive was dead. Marge cried as they took her away, but she cried tears of joy. The doctor signed the death certificate. 1 Olive had died of a heart attack; there was no mention of poison. 160

Alfred and Marge were married a few months after Olive's death. They often talked about how they got rid of Olive, especially after their bedtime drink. The small tin of poison was given a place on the kitchen shelf, where its label 2 could be seen by all. 165

It read, 'Concentrated 3 Powdered Milk'.

1. **death certificate** : a document proving that a person is dead.
2. **label** : piece of paper on the tin that described the contents.
3. **concentrated** : made stronger by having some water removed.

After reading

1 **What can you remember about the story?**

a. Marge and Olive's age ....

b. The eldest sister ....

c. Marge's illness ....

d. Marge's favourite food ....

e. Marge and Alfred's secret meeting place ....

f. What Alfred and Marge talked about ....

g. The presents Alfred bought ....

h. What the sisters had for breakfast ....

i. Why Marge didn't eat that evening ....

j. How Olive died ....

k. When Alfred and Marge got married ....

l. What was put on the kitchen shelf ....

2 **Who/what do the underlined words refer to?**

a. When <u>their</u> father died.

b. Marge was afraid of <u>her</u>.

c. <u>They</u> were so expensive.

d. She couldn't eat <u>these things</u>.

e. <u>It</u> had all been a mistake.

f. She'd miss <u>them</u> too.

g. Olive did not find <u>them</u>.

h. Give me the other <u>one</u>.

i. When <u>it</u> arrived ...

j. It read ...

3 **Rearrange the words to make complete sentences.**

a. before Second met the Alfred War World Marge

....

b. letters Olive read Marge's always

....

c. left money a Olive's and father Marge lot of

....

d. had desertion accused been of Alfred

....

e. handbag hid Marge the in tin letter her the and

....

f. Marge ambulance and telephone picked an called up the

....

4 **How good is your vocabulary? Choose the correct definitions.**

1. temper
   a. anger.
   b. a pencil.
   c. a river.

2. a mistake
   a. a headache.
   b. an error.
   c. a cake.

3. a genius
   a. a character in Aladin.
   b. a very clever person.
   c. a banknote.

4. a meatloaf
   a. bread.
   b. a dish made of meat.
   c. a sweet.

5. to sniff
   a. to have a cold.
   b. to smell.
   c. to taste.

6. angina
   a. a flower.
   b. a dance.
   c. an illness.

7. tin
   a. a small car.
   b. a container made of metal.
   c. a toy.

8. cellar
   a. salt.
   b. a room underground.
   c. a bird.

9. to sign
   a. to write your name.
   b. to draw.
   c. to sing a song.

10. a tablet
   a. a pill.
   b. a type of table.
   c. a blackboard.

11. price
   a. sound.
   b. cost.
   c. fruit.

12. poison
   a. a drink.
   b. food.
   c. a very dangerous substance.

5 Complete the sentences with the words in the box.

than	to	for	of	on	about

a. Marge was afraid .... Olive.

b. Olive was a little bit older .... Marge.

c. Olive liked going shopping .... her own.

d. Olive often talked .... the price of clothes.

e. Alfred asked Marge .... marry him.

f. Olive ordered Marge to make her a cup .... tea.

g. After a while Marge called .... an ambulance.

6 Here is a page from Marge's diary. There are 10 grammatical mistakes in it – can you correct them?

MONDAY **22** September

At last Alfred and I is happy! Olive dead
last month and we had his funeral a week
later. Now Alfred and I can get marry.
We goed into town yesterday to do some
shopping – I bought meself a beautiful pink
dress and Alfred buyed some new shoes.
We hope to get married in a few month time
and then go to the seaside for ours
honeymoon. I sometimes miss Olive and her
strange ways but I think I prefer to live
with Alfred – he love me so much ...

1. ....

2. ....

3. ....

4. ....

5. ....

6. ....

7. ....

8. ....

9. ....

10. ....

Listening

1 **Who did what? Olive (O), Marge (M) or Alfred (A).**
Listen to the story and then without looking at the
text tick (✓) accordingly:

	O	M	A
a. paid the bills	☐	☐	☐
b. got the slippers	☐	☐	☐
c. made the tea	☐	☐	☐
d. left the town	☐	☐	☐
e. sang together	☐	☐	☐
f. made breakfast	☐	☐	☐
g. bought the poison	☐	☐	☐
h. took tablets	☐	☐	☐

Now listen again and check your answers.

2 **Listen to ll. 1-10 and fill in the following gaps.**

Marge and Olive were two sisters who .... lived together all
.... lives. They were both .... seventy. When their father
died leaving .... the house and some money, it was Olive who
was the boss. She was a .... older than Marge and had a very
bad .... Marge was afraid of her, and soon .... to do
everything she was told to do. Olive did the shopping, paid the
.............., gas and water bills, and decided how to spend their
money. Marge did the ...., the cooking and decided when to
put the .... out to be collected.

Simpson's Buried Treasure

Before reading

1 **Answer the following questions:**

- Have you ever found any money?

....

- Where did you find it?

....

- How much did you find?

....

- Have you ever found anything strange or unusual?

....

2 **Which word is the odd one out? Why?**

a. grass   tree   lawn   spade

....

b. rain   thunder   sun   hot

....

c. stupid   strong   cry   heavy

....

3 **Look through the first part of the story (ll. 1-10) quickly and look for the following information:**

a. How many boys are there?

....

b. What are their names?

....

c. Where are they at the beginning of the story?

....

Simpson's Buried

Treasure

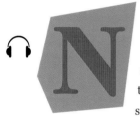

Nicholas walked slowly down the narrow country road holding the dirty piece of paper tightly [1] in his hand. In the distance he could see Buster standing against the wall, smoking a cigarette. Nicholas was frightened. He knew he was in Buster's territory [2] and that Buster would probably hit him for being there. As usual, Buster was not alone. Lewis and Driscoll, two of his closest friends, stood waiting for orders. Nicholas knew he was in trouble. Buster always wanted to show that he was the boss.

'Look, there's Rabbit!'

Nicholas stopped suddenly as the three boys ran towards him. Buster threw down his cigarette. He blew the last of the smoke into Nicholas's face.

1. **tightly** : firmly.
2. **territory** : (here) an area of land belonging to a person.

15 'Are you deaf, or just stupid, eh Rabbit?'

Nicholas coughed as the disgusting [1] smoke filled his nostrils. [2] He felt a sudden blow [3] to the side of his face. His cheek hurt and he wanted to cry but he made himself stop.

'You're trespassing, [4] Rabbit!' Driscoll continued. I've told 20 you to keep away from here.'

The boys surrounded him, and a heavy hand pushed him to the ground. Nicholas covered his head with his arms and closed his eyes, waiting for the blows.

'What's this?'

25 'Looks like a map.'

'That's old Simpson's garden!'

'Yeah! But what are all those crosses for?'

Nicholas opened his eyes and lifted his head. Buster was holding the piece of paper he had dropped.

30 'Hey Rabbit! Whose map is this? What's it for?' Buster grabbed Nicholas by the arm, and pulled him up. Nicholas kept his head down and didn't answer.

'Come on, tell me before I...!' Buster pushed Nicholas against the wall.

35 'Okay, okay! It's a map of Simpson's garden,' he answered reluctantly. [5]

1. **disgusting** : extremely unpleasant.

2. **nostrils** :

3. **blow** : hard stroke (given with a hand/stick).

4. **trespassing** : entering private property without permission.

5. **reluctantly** : unwillingly.

SimPson's Buried TreasurE

'I can see that, you idiot. [1] What are you doing with it?'

Once again Nicholas refused to speak. The three bullies [2] stood over him, and he knew that they were waiting for an answer.

'It's a map of Simpson's buried treasure, but it's only a legend. Nobody believes that it really exists,' he said.

'Ah, no. Then where were you going?' Lewis replied.

'Yeah! That's why you had the nerve [3] to pass through here! You're hoping to find the treasure yourself.

'I've heard about that treasure,' added Driscoll. 'They say that old Simpson buried a fortune in his garden before he died.'

'Oh, no! It's only a legend. Nobody really believes that story'. Another blow made Nicholas fall to the ground. His arm ached.

'Shut up! I'll be the judge of that!' Buster said, smiling to the others. 'Now, get lost!' [4]

Nicholas stood up and moved away.

'Go on, run!' Lewis yelled, [5] laughing.

Nicholas ran as fast as he could. Laughter and cries of 'run rabbit run' came from behind him.

Once he'd turned the corner, he stopped to catch his

---

1. **idiot** : a stupid person.
2. **bullies** : (singular: "bully") people who hurt or frighten weaker people.
3. **nerve** : bravery.
4. **get lost** : go away.
5. **yelled** : shouted loudly.

breath, and waited. As expected, the three boys were walking
60 towards old Simpson's house chatting together excitedly. They
didn't know that Nicholas was following them!

When the small group entered the garden, Nicholas crept
into a large hole in the hedge [1] of the house next door. Here,
he could watch the boys without the risk of being discovered.

65 'Oh no!' Buster exclaimed, his face falling. The garden was
really overgrown with grass and weeds [2] everywhere.

'How can we dig for treasure if we can't see where we are
digging?' Lewis asked, kicking at some weeds.

'We'll have to cut the grass first,' Buster announced.
70 'You two go and get some gardening tools and a
lawn mower. [3] Don't forget the spades.' [4]

Lewis and Driscoll disappeared and
left Buster alone in the garden.
Nicholas knelt down to rest his
75 tired legs, and prepared himself
for a long wait. The wind blew
through the hedge, and a large
grey cloud blocked out the last rays of
the sun. He looked up and realized that it was going to rain.

---

1. **hedge** : a row of small trees planted close together.
2. **weeds** : wild plants growing where not wanted.
3. **lawn mower** ; a machine for cutting grass
4. **spades** :

80   'Come on!' Buster exclaimed, as the two boys struggled [1] through the wooden gate with their equipment. 'I'll start mowing, you two can clear up [2] the grass,' he ordered, pushing the heavy mower onto the untidy lawn.

   Nicholas watched patiently as the bullies worked. The
85 rhythmic sound of the lawn mower, and the sweet smell of freshly cut grass was quite pleasant.

   The first drops of rain made them work faster, and they hardly spoke as they carried on working.

   'Leave the grass over there in the corner.' Buster shouted
90 over the noise of the howling [3] wind. 'Hurry up! There's going to be a storm.'

   He had hardly finished the sentence, when a loud noise startled [4] all four of them – thunder! [5] Large drops of rain fell heavily, soaking them to the skin [6] instantly. All except
95 Nicholas. The thick hedge provided an excellent shelter, [7] and he enjoyed watching the three boys struggling with their spades, and following the instructions on the map.

   'Have you found anything?' Lewis shouted, wiping [8] his face with a damp [9] sleeve.

1. **struggled** : had difficulty carrying the tools.
2. **clear up** : tidy up.
3. **howling** : blowing hard, making a loud noise.
4. **startled** : frightened.
5. **thunder** : loud sound in the sky during a storm.
6. **soaking them to the skin** : making them very, very wet.
7. **shelter** : cover.
8. **wiping** : cleaning by rubbing.
9. **damp** : a bit wet.

'No! What about you, Driscoll?' Buster replied. 100

'Nothing, and I've dug three holes already! I'm really wet!'

'Me too!'

The wet earth became heavier by the minute and Buster was getting tired.

'This stupid spade won't come out of the mud,' he cried. 105 He was getting angrier and angrier. To the relief [1] of his friends, he shouted, 'Let's get out of here! It's obvious [2] that the treasure doesn't exist!'

As he turned to go, he stumbled [3] over one of the holes that he'd dug. 110

'Aaargh!'

Nicholas covered his mouth with his hand. The sight of Buster lying on the ground with his face covered with mud was more than he'd expected. He started laughing uncontrollably. He knew that he couldn't be heard above the 115 noise of the rain.

He watched as the boys, arguing amongst themselves, collected up their tools, and left the garden. Nicholas couldn't stop laughing.

As suddenly as it had started, the rain stopped. Nicholas 120 crawled [4] out of his hiding place. He looked round the garden. It was wet, but very tidy. In his haste, [5] Buster had forgotten

---

1. **relief** : a feeling of comfort that something disgusting has ended.
2. **obvious** : clear.
3. **stumbled** : fell.
4. **crawled** : moved slowly on his hands and knees.
5. **In his haste** : In the hurry.

his spade and had left it sticking out of the ground. Nicholas
jumped over the hedge to get it, then ran to the front of the
125 house and waited.

Finally, the grey clouds disappeared, and the sun came out.
A blue car which Nicholas recognized immediately,
approached slowly, stopping outside old Simpson's house.
The driver, a tall, smart woman with red hair, stepped out of
130 the car and walked towards him.

'Nicholas', she called, looking at the muddy spade and
smiling. 'Don't tell me that you've already done that job we
talked about? You haven't tidied up the garden already, have
you?'

135 'Yes, Miss Simpson,' Nicholas replied, wiping his forehead
and sighing.¹ The woman walked around to the back of the
garden.

'Good Lord!² What a wonderful job you've done! And in the
rain, too. You poor thing,' she continued, putting a hand on
140 his shoulder. 'And you've even dug the holes for my rose
bushes, exactly where I wanted them!' she exclaimed.

Without hesitation ³ she put her hand into her shoulder
bag, and pulled out a small purse.

'Let me pay you at once. I didn't expect you to do such a
145 good job. And all on your own, too!'

---

1. **sighing** : (here) breathing out slowly to show tiredness.
2. **Good Lord!** : expression of surprise.
3. **without hesitation** : without delay.

SimPson's Buried TreasurE

She took out one, two, then three £5 notes from her purse. Nicholas gasped. [1]

'But Miss Simpson...' he pretended to be surprised.

'Oh, no. I insist. Take it, you've done a very good job.'

Thanking her again and again, Nicholas accepted the 150 money and turned to go home. He knew that he would have to avoid [2] Buster for a while. Fortunately for him, a bad cold would keep Buster out of the way for a long time.

---

1. **gasped** : took in his breath suddenly because of surprise.
2. **avoid** : keep away from.

After reading

1 **Are the following sentences true (T) or false (F)?**

		T	F
a.	Nicholas met the boys in Simpson's garden.	☐	☐
b.	Buster was with two of his friends.	☐	☐
c.	Buster was the leader.	☐	☐
d.	Buster hit Nicholas three times.	☐	☐
e.	There was a rabbit running in the field.	☐	☐
f.	Nicholas hid in the house.	☐	☐
g.	The boys cleaned the garden before digging.	☐	☐
h.	Buster found the treasure.	☐	☐
i.	Miss Simpson owned the garden.	☐	☐
j.	Miss Simpson paid Nicholas for watching the boys.	☐	☐

Now correct the false sentences.

....

....

....

....

....

....

....

2 **A** The pictures below are scenes from the story – but they are all mixed up. Can you put them into the correct order? (Don't complete the sentences yet!)

a ☐

The boys .... into the garden.

b ☐

Buster and his friends .... working.

c ☐

Nicholas .... Buster and his friends.

d ☐

Miss Simpson .... Nicholas some money.

e ☐

Buster .... Nicholas across the face.

f ☐

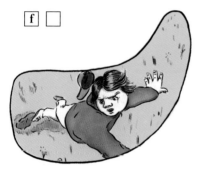

It started raining and Buster .... into a hole.

g ☐

The boys .... the garden.

h ☐

Nicholas .... behind a hedge.

i ☐

Miss Simpson .... in her car.

B   **Now put the correct form of the verbs (Simple Past) into the gaps.**

| meet | hit | go | hide | start | fall | leave | arrive | give |

3 Can you match the words with the correct definitions? (All the words are in the story.)

a. stupid	part of the body
b. legend	shout loudly
c. spade	not very intelligent
d. stumble	a very old story
e. wet	a tool used for digging
f. yell	not dry
g. face	fall over

4 **A** All these things are usually found in the garden or in the countryside. Can you solve the anagrams? 1 Use the pictures to help you.

a. deesw ....

b. olto ....

c. omewlarnw ....

d. despa ....

e. gedhe ....

f. ragss ....

g. busrhsoe ....

1. **anagrams** : (here) words made by letters in a different order.

B   Now can you find them in this word grid?

G	D	R	R	S	T	Z	H	K
L	A	W	N	M	O	W	E	R
T	R	E	E	L	O	E	D	H
M	D	G	P	P	L	E	G	Q
U	X	R	S	P	A	D	E	V
D	Y	A	F	D	E	S	O	O
Y	U	S	Q	P	U	I	C	H
R	O	S	E	B	U	S	H	J

5 A   Complete the chart below.

a. tall	taller	tallest
b. cold	....	....
c. young	....	....
d. rich	....	....
e. fat	....	....
f. hot	....	....
g. wet	....	....
h. thin	....	....
i. happy	....	....
j. small	....	....
k. good	....	....
l. bad	....	....
m. intelligent	....	....
n. beautiful	....	....

B Now using the adjectives from 5A, write a sentence about each boy using the superlative. The pictures will help you.

  a. Buster always eats lots of cakes, sweets and chocolate.

  He's ....

  b. Nicholas has got a lot of money.

  He's ....

  c. Buster is 1m 65, Driscoll is 1m 63 and Lewis is 1m 70.

  Lewis is ....

  d. Driscoll looks younger than his age because he's not very tall.

  ....

6 This is a map of the country village where the boys live. Read the directions on the next page and put the symbols from the key in the places on the map.

Go straight up the road. Take the second road on the left – there's a chemists' on the corner. Go down this road until you come to the bridge. Take the first left after the bridge. When you come to a pub called 'The Cock and Bull' turn right and then second left. At the end of this road turn left again. After about 200 metres you'll come to some traffic lights. Nicholas lives in the house on the right after the traffic lights.

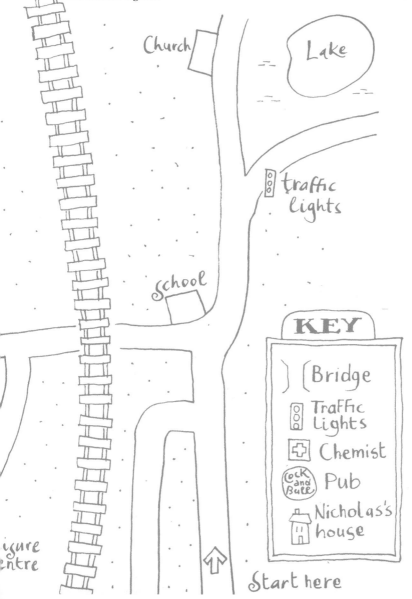

7 Complete the following clues.

    a. Longest part of the body ....

    b. You write with this ....

    c. It's in the middle of your face ....

    d. They can be blue, green or brown ....

    e. You eat, speak and kiss with this ....

    f. We usually have 32 ....

    g. The plural form is irregular ....

    h. You hear with these ....

    i. The top part of the body ....

    j. It joins the head to the body ....

    k. Part of face above eyebrows ....

    l. Your arms are attached to these ....

Use your dictionary to find out about the other parts of the body you don't know.

....

....

....

....

....

....

Listening

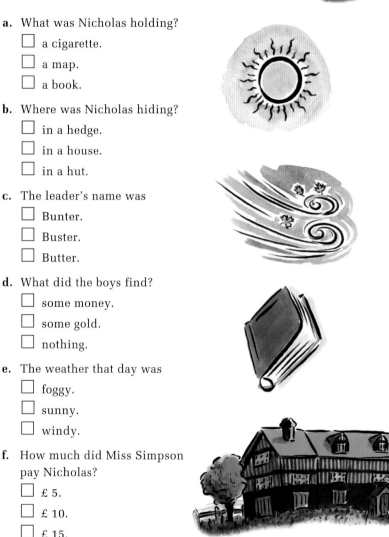

1 Read the following questions. Then try and find the answers by listening to the story.

a. What was Nicholas holding?
- ☐ a cigarette.
- ☐ a map.
- ☐ a book.

b. Where was Nicholas hiding?
- ☐ in a hedge.
- ☐ in a house.
- ☐ in a hut.

c. The leader's name was
- ☐ Bunter.
- ☐ Buster.
- ☐ Butter.

d. What did the boys find?
- ☐ some money.
- ☐ some gold.
- ☐ nothing.

e. The weather that day was
- ☐ foggy.
- ☐ sunny.
- ☐ windy.

f. How much did Miss Simpson pay Nicholas?
- ☐ £ 5.
- ☐ £ 10.
- ☐ £ 15.

113

2 Who said what? After listening to the story decide whether the following sentences refer to Buster (B), Nicholas (N), Lewis (L), Driscoll (D) or Miss Simpson (S).

		B	N	L	D	S
a.	'Are you deaf or just stupid?'	☐	☐	☐	☐	☐
b.	'I'm really wet.'	☐	☐	☐	☐	☐
c.	'You've done a very good job.'	☐	☐	☐	☐	☐
d.	'Run, rabbit, run.'	☐	☐	☐	☐	☐
e.	'Don't forget the spades.'	☐	☐	☐	☐	☐
f.	'It's a map of Simpson's garden.'	☐	☐	☐	☐	☐
g.	'You're trespassing.'	☐	☐	☐	☐	☐
h.	'Good Lord!'	☐	☐	☐	☐	☐

I'm really wet.

It's a map of Simpson's garden.

Are you deaf or just stupid?

You're trespassing.

You've done a very good job.

Run, rabbit, run.

Don't forget the spades.

Good Lord!

A Strange Case

Before reading

1 **How superstitious ¹ are you? Do you believe in fate?**

	YES	NO
• Have you got a lucky number?	☐	☐
What is it?		
• Do you often read your horoscope ² in magazines?	☐	☐
How often?		
• Do you think it's unlucky to walk under a ladder?	☐	☐
• If you see a black cat do you think it's lucky?	☐	☐
• Have you ever been to a fortune teller?	☐	☐
What did they say?		
• Do you believe in ghosts?	☐	☐
• Do you think Friday, 13th is unlucky?	☐	☐
• Do you think dreams foretell the future?	☐	☐
• Have you got a lucky object?	☐	☐
What is it?		

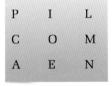

2 **Write three things you are frightened of:**

....

....

....

3 **How many words can you find in the box? Give yourself a time limit
– 10 minutes. There is also a nine-letter word. Can you guess what it is?**

P	I	L
C	O	M
A	E	N

1. **superstitious** : not based on human reason or science.
2. **horoscope** : forecast of a person's future based on the positions of stars.

116

A Strange Case

s a police detective, I've seen and heard many strange and unusual things. I suppose that after forty years of service this is only to be expected. However, I thought nothing could surprise me... That was until I met Mr Perch! 5

Poor old Perch – a tall, elegant man. I'll never forget him. When he came to the police station one morning and told me his incredible[1] story, I confess,[2] I thought he was senile.[3] He told me that he was going to be murdered[4] – later that night. I thought that he had invented the story just to get some 10 attention, and this made me feel sorry for him. There was something about him that reminded me of my Uncle Henry.

---

1. **incredible** : hard to believe.
2. **confess** : admit.
3. **senile** : not very clever because of old age.
4. **murdered** : killed by a person intentionally.

They had the same walk and the same way of speaking. Clear and precise. [1] I couldn't send him away. It was almost lunch time so I asked him to stay for a while and chat.

He was an intelligent man. We talked about all sorts of things. Politics, the Second World War, even the weather. I remember wondering [2] why a man like him had become obsessed with [3] this idea of murder. When he told me that he was a widower, [4] I understood. He also had no children and no relatives. He was completely alone. I offered him a cup of coffee but he refused. He said that he had to go, but first he made me promise not to look for his murderer. He added that his wife had appeared to him in a dream and had told him what was going to happen to him. I asked him if he wanted protection and promised to send him someone later that evening. When he refused, I lost my patience! I had enough cases to solve without worrying about crimes that had not yet been committed. [5] Perch stood up and turned to leave. He said that he did not want protection – he was looking forward to [6] seeing his wife again. He was so convincing that I almost believed him.

Through the glass door I could see Marshall coming towards my office. He was holding the report that I was

1. **precise** : exact.
2. **wondering** : asking myself.
3. **become obsessed with** : become too interested in.
4. **widower** ; a man whose wife has died.
5. **committed** : 'to commit a crime' means to do something illegal.
6. **looking forward to** : feeling excited and pleased about something that is going to happen.

A Strange Case

waiting for. I signalled for him to wait outside, then I   35
accompanied Perch to the door. He kept repeating that after
his death he did not want us to look for the murderer. It was a
waste of time, he said. The criminal would get the punishment
that he deserved.

As I opened the door, I asked him why. Why should   40
someone want to murder him? Did he have any enemies?

When he pulled out a thick wad [1] of banknotes
from his pocket, I was shocked. I told him
that he was looking for trouble and
advised him to go to the bank and
deposit [2] the money before he went
home. He just laughed...

The last thing he said before leaving
was, 'man cannot change his destiny.'[3]

I watched him leave, and wondered if I would ever see him   50
again. When Marshall came into my office, I told him about
Perch's visit. Marshall was new and did not have much
experience. I thought he would laugh at Perch's story, but he
didn't. He seemed quite worried. He asked me for the old
man's address, and offered to go and see if he needed   55
anything. I was surprised and pleased at his offer, but I didn't
really think it was necessary for him to go and see Perch.

---

1. **wad** : large amount of notes pressed together.
2. **deposit** : store.
3. **destiny** : things that will happen in future.

Work kept me busy for most of the day, and I forget about Perch's visit. When I received the phone call in the early
60 hours of the morning, I knew that Perch was involved. A boy walking his dog had found a body. I rushed to the scene of the crime and discovered that it was old Perch. He'd been hit on the back of the head with a heavy object, just a few metres away from his home. I'll never forget the expression on his
65 face. His lips smiled and he looked happy. I like to think that he had met his wife after all.

The money that he'd shown me had been stolen – the thief had also taken his wedding ring. A voice in my head kept saying, "you see, I told you so!"
70 Even though I had promised Perch not to look for the murderer, I had to do my job. Besides, I wanted to find the criminal and make him pay for what he had done.

I spent all morning looking through the computer files for possible suspects, and I found plenty. It was such an easy job
75 robbing an old man – it could have been anyone!

Marshall wanted to go and pay them a visit that very day, but I was tired. I had a headache and I couldn't stop thinking of Perch and the tragic ¹ way he had died. I considered myself

---

1. **tragic** : very sad.

responsible. If only I had accompanied him home... If only I had convinced him to take the money to the bank...   80

If only...

Marshall and I questioned a few of our suspects. They all seemed to have an alibi [1] so nobody was arrested. Marshall was especially interested in finding the criminal. The death of the old man seemed to trouble him in some way.   85

Days passed and we were getting nowhere. I had taken this particular case to heart [2] and one day I even dreamt of old Perch. He was sitting on a park bench, next to a pleasant looking woman. I presumed that this was his wife. He lifted a hand and pointed at me.   90

'Remember your promise!' he said. 'The thief will be punished. Have patience.'

As in all dreams, I woke up before I had a chance to answer him. The next morning I had an appointment with Marshall at the office. As I sat waiting I heard a voice in my ear.   95

'Detective Galloway, don't forget your promise!'

It was Perch's voice. I turned around expecting to find someone behind me, but there was nobody there.

I was under pressure and I needed to solve this case in a hurry!   100

Three days had passed since Perch's death. I had plenty of work to keep me occupied,[3] but I could not stop thinking about

1. **alibi** : proof that a suspect is in another place when a crime happens.
2. **to heart** : personally.
3. **occupied** : busy.

A StrAnge CaSe

old Perch. It was half past ten when
Marshall arrived bringing me my
mid-morning coffee and sandwiches.
I wasn't hungry so I told him to take a
break [1] himself.

We talked about Perch. There was
something that I hadn't told Marshall.
Perch had shown me a note he had written for me and had   110
wrapped it around the wad of money. In this, he explained
how the thief would be punished.

I was about to tell him about this when he said something
that puzzled me. He said that he didn't think the thief would
get the punishment that Perch had predicted – it was unlikely   115
for someone to choke [2] on a piece of bread... Exactly what
Perch had written in his note! How did Marshall know about
this? Unless he was the murderer...

He sat in front of me calmly eating the sandwiches. I stood
up and demanded to know who had given him this   120
information. When had he seen the note? His face grew white
and he realized that he had made a mistake. He tried to find
an excuse, then he suddenly started to cough. I waited for him
to stop but he didn't. He just carried on coughing and gasping
for breath. [3] I didn't know what to do. I tried hitting him hard   125

---

1. **break** : rest.
2. **choke** : stop breathing because of something in the throat.
3. **gasping for breath** : having difficulty in breathing.

on the back, but it was no use. I rushed to the office door and called for Patterson and Taylor. By the time they reached the office, Marshall lay on the floor. He was already blue in the face. Patterson pulled him to his feet, and I watched helplessly
130   as they tried to force the piece of bread out of his throat. Yes, the piece of bread that Perch had warned me about!

Unfortunately for Marshall, there was nothing that could be done to save him. Patterson lowered him to the ground and we called
135   the coroner. [1] I suddenly felt ill.

After Marshall's death, I made a few enquiries. Marshall had been a gambler. [2] He had lost a lot of money in a poker game, and had got into bad
140   company. [3] He had a long list of debts to pay and some of his creditors [4] were dangerous people. When he had seen the wad of notes that Perch carried about with him, he could not resist the opportunity of getting himself out of trouble. His uniform did not mean much to him
145   – he was only interested in himself. This explained his concern and the reason why he was so interested in the case.

The case had been solved without any help from me or my colleagues! Perch had been right, and now he could rest in peace.

1. **coroner** : official who enquires into the cause of death.
2. **gambler** : person who spends money playing games in order to win more money.
3. **had got into bad company** : had made friends with bad people.
4. **creditors** : people to whom money is owed.

After reading

1 **Choose the correct answer.**

    a. The detective first met Perch
- ☐ in the evening.
- ☐ in the afternoon.
- ☐ in the morning.

    b. Perch stayed in the office and had
- ☐ a drink.
- ☐ a chat.
- ☐ a sandwich.

    c. Perch was murdered because he had
- ☐ lots of enemies.
- ☐ lots of money.
- ☐ lots of friends.

    d. The body was found
- ☐ in a field.
- ☐ near Perch's home.
- ☐ in Perch's living room.

    e. Perch's body was found by
- ☐ a dog.
- ☐ a young boy.
- ☐ the police.

f. The murderer was discovered by

☐ Detective Galloway.

☐ Marshall.

☐ Patterson and Taylor.

g. Marshall stole the money because

☐ he wanted to go on holiday.

☐ he wanted to go and play cards.

☐ he had money problems.

2 **A** **Choose the correct plural form.**

a. daisys	daisyes	daisies
b. eyes	eies	eye
c. mens	mans	men
d. noises	noisys	noisyes
e. watchs	watches	waches
f. wifes	wives	wifs
g. mouses	mices	mice
h. forks	forkes	fork
i. machs	matches	matchs

B **What's the plural of:**

a. child ....

b. foot ....

c. woman ....

d. person ....

e. tooth ,,,,,,,,,,,,,,

f. trousers ....

g. jeans ....

h. rat ....

i. penny ....

j. man ....

k. knifo ....

l. glasses ....

126

3 Put the following words into the correct column (refer to the story).

> widower   meet   hard   intelligent   towards   his
> into   chat   body   calmly   old   at   search   bread
> helplessly   our   behind   wonder   in front of

Adjective	Preposition	Verb	Noun	Adverb
....	....	....	....	....
....	....	....	....	....
....	....	....	....	....
....	....	....		
	....			

4 Find the Simple Past of these irregular verbs in the word square. All the verbs are in the story.

> stand   hear   wake   make   tell   send   see   keep
> find   hit   be   have   meet   grow   feel   lose   go

S	A	W	N	A	D	F	G	H	T
M	E	W	H	I	T	O	M	E	T
A	K	E	P	T	M	U	I	A	O
D	S	E	N	T	V	N	L	R	L
E	W	F	E	L	T	D	W	D	D
S	T	O	O	D	Z	E	E	A	P
N	X	Z	L	O	S	T	P	Y	S
P	B	G	R	E	W	W	E	N	T
W	O	K	E	U	H	A	D	Z	Q

5 CROSSWORD

Across

4. Past tense of 'read'
5. Perch was murdered in the early hours of the ....
8. Go .... school; go .... the cinema; go .... the park
10. I, you, she, he, ..., we, you, they
11. Opposite of 'young'
12. A pain in the head
14. The Inspector received this one morning
16. It is sometimes the colour of the sky and the sea
19. Watch a film, see a rainbow but .... at a picture
20. Marshall was one of these
23. Part of the face
24. Perch did not have any friends or relatives. He was <u>lneao</u>.

Down

1. A pet
2. A number before two
3. Abbreviation [1] for morning
6. When they found the body, there was .... in the pockets
7. Past tense of 'take'
8. I don't like coffee, I prefer ....
9. Something you do when you sleep
13. Opposite of 'alive'
14. Perch went to the .... for help
15. It's cold in here – close the <u>rodo</u>
17. Pavarotti is famous for his ....
18. Not very well
21. If you put water into the freezer it turns into this
22. Would you like a cup of tea? ...., thanks.

1. **abbreviation** : short form.

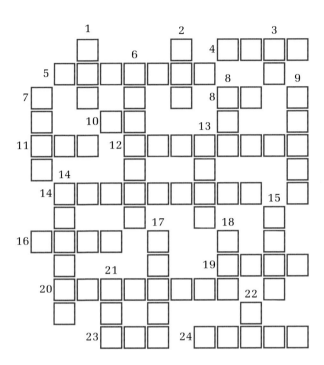

Listening

1 **A** **Listen to the story and decide which sentence is true (T) or false (F). Correct the false ones.**

	T	F
a. Perch reminded the Inspector of his uncle.	☐	☐
b. They talked about Uncle Henry.	☐	☐
c. Perch was not worried about dying.	☐	☐
d. The thief only stole his money.	☐	☐

    e. The Inspector worked on the case all morning. ☐ ☐

    f. Marshall was a friend of Mr Perch's. ☐ ☐

    g. The Inspector knew how the murderer
        was going to die. ☐ ☐

    h. Marshall choked on a piece of cake. ☐ ☐

B Now complete the summary.

One day a man called Mr .... came to see me in the police

station. He had a very strange .... to tell. He said he was going

to be murdered very near in the future but he did not want me to look

for his .... I told Marshall, another police officer, about the

visit and then carried on working. The next .... I heard that

Perch was dead and that his money and wedding .... had been

stolen. I started to look for the murderer with .... help.

.... days later I was with Marshall in my office – it was

lunchtime and we were having a cup of .... and eating some

.... We were discussing Perch's case when Marshall said

something that made me very suspicious. Suddenly he

started............... on his sandwich. He died exactly how Perch had

predicted – choking on a piece of ....

TEST   YOUR   MEMORY

Now that you have read all the stories. How much can you remember?

1. What was Trudy's problem?

   ....

2. Why did the butler leave Cranberry?

   ....

3. What were the crosses on Simpson's map?

   ....

4. Who got promotion?

   ....

5. What was in the fridge?

   ....

6. How did Ian get to Littlepoint?

   ....

7. Why was Madame Eve's living room empty?

   ....

8. How did Olive die?

   ....

9. Who found Mr Perch's body?

   ....

10. Name the characters in "Simpson's Buried Treasure".

    ....

11. Name three things Marge liked eating.

    ....

12. How did Perch know he was going to die?

    ....

13. What was the 'little black object'?

....

14. Nicholas's nickname.

....

15. Who was Trudy's boyfriend?

....

16. When was Perch's body discovered?

....

17. How old were Marge and Olive?

....

18. What did Cranberry bury?

....

19. How did Marshall die?

....

20. How many letters did Trudy write to Susan?

....

21. How did Ian get to Cliffview?

....

22. What is the colour of Miss Simpson's hair?

....

23. Where did Madame Eve live?

....

24. Who was Alfred?

....

Which story do you like best? Why?

••

EXIT TEST

Are the following sentences true (T) or false (F)? Correct the false ones.

A Case of Trust   T   F

a. John Baker wanted to see Detective Miller. ☐ ☐

b. Baker was pleased at the possibility of promotion. ☐ ☐

c. William Cranberry asked his butler to take him to the ☐ ☐
bookshop for a copy of *Strange Destiny*.

d. When he opened the book, William Cranberry found ☐ ☐
a receipt from the local pawnshop inside.

e. When he went to see the clairvoyant he was amazed ☐ ☐
at all the information she knew about him.

f. William Cranberry put the small, antique, silver ☐ ☐
mirror in his mother's grave.

g. Baker realised that Madame Eve and Jenkins had ☐ ☐
planned the theft together.

h. Baker got the promotion in the end. ☐ ☐

The Penfriend   T   F

a. Trudy's parents allowed her to go to the party with ☐ ☐
Tony but she had to be home by nine o'clock.

b. Trudy's penfriend was called Susan. ☐ ☐

c. After writing to Susan, Trudy's relationship with her ☐ ☐
parents got worse.

d. Trudy was so worried about Susan that she told Tony ☐ ☐
about her and showed him Susan's letters.

e. Trudy's mother's friend was a social worker. ☐ ☐

f. Susan was of the same age as Trudy. ☐ ☐

g. Maggie helped Susan to find somewhere to live. ☐ ☐

h. Both Trudy and Susan are much happier now. ☐ ☐

The Big Mistake

	T	F
a. Ian was going to stay at his uncle's house in Littlepoint.	☐	☐
b. Ian had a big meal that evening.	☐	☐
c. Ian was excited when he heard the thieves talking.	☐	☐
d. One man had a wine-stain on his shirt.	☐	☐
e. The police arrived and Ian was arrested.	☐	☐
f. The number of his uncle's house was twenty-eight.	☐	☐
g. The two men had run over another man.	☐	☐

Marge and Olive

	T	F
a. Marge and Olive were under seventy.	☐	☐
b. Marge was the boss.	☐	☐
c. Marge loved shopping days.	☐	☐
d. Olive always agreed to buy cheese, milk and yoghurt for Marge.	☐	☐
e. Marge was very happy when Alfred returned to town.	☐	☐
f. Olive and Alfred planned to get married.	☐	☐
g. Olive died of a heart attack.	☐	☐

Simpson's Buried Treasure   T   F

a. Buster called Nicholas 'Bunny'. ☐ ☐

b. Nicholas had a map of Simpson's garden. ☐ ☐

c. Buster and his friends cut the grass in
Simpson's garden. ☐ ☐

d. The treasure was buried in the ground. ☐ ☐

e. Buster fell into a hole. ☐ ☐

f. Buster and his friends got paid for digging up
the garden so well. ☐ ☐

g. Nicholas received £10 from Miss Simpson. ☐ ☐

A Strange Case   T   F

a. Mr Perch was a short man. ☐ ☐

b. He made the police detective promise not to look for
his murderer. ☐ ☐

c. Mr Perch's body was found early in the evening. ☐ ☐

d. The police detective tried to keep his promise to
Mr Perch. ☐ ☐

e. The murderer choked on a piece of meat. ☐ ☐

f. Marshall had been a gambler. ☐ ☐

The Big Mistake and Other Stories

KEY TO THE ACTIVITIES

A CASE OF TRUST

Before reading (page 10)

1. Open answers.

2. **Parts of the body:** hand; throat; brain; shoulders.
   Food: sandwiches; coffee.
   Weather: no examples in the story.
   Furniture: chair; desk; bookshelves.
   Buildings: library; pawnshop; house; bank.

After reading (page 22)

1. a. Miller wanted Baker to solve a case.
   b. To get a book called *Strange Destiny*.
   c. A receipt from a local pawnshop.
   d. He thought that a clairvoyant could help him solve his business problems.
   e. Twice.
   f. A few days after he had buried his great-grandmother's necklace.

2. a. Baker
   b. Jenkins
   c. Cranberry
   d. Madame Eve
   e. Madame Eve
   f. Jenkins
   g. Cranberry
   h. Jenkins
   i. Baker
   j. Cranberry

3. a. Cranberry is leaving **for** Cortina tomorrow.
   b. The library is **at** the end **of** this road.
   c. Jenkins waited **for** Cranberry in the car.
   d. The book was **on** the top shelf. The librarian climbed **up** the step-ladder to get it.

   e. Did Cranberry believe **in** the supernatural?
   f. When Baker walked **into** the room, Miller was waiting.

4. b. clever — intelligent
   c. ghost — spirit
   d. inquisitive — curious
   e. anxious — worried
   f. very old — antique
   g. broken — damaged
   h. position — place
   i. confidential — private
   j. persuade — convince
   k. space — room
   l. reply — answer
   m. destiny — fate

5. a. Miller asked Baker to solve the mystery **because** he wanted promotion.
   b. Baker read the report **and** solved the mystery.
   c. Cranberry dug up his mother's grave **but** couldn't find the necklace.
   d. Jenkins left Cranberry **because** his mother was very ill.
   e. Cranberry had no proof **so** he didn't go to the police.
   f. Baker took some money out of the bank **and** went on holiday.
   g. Cranberry wanted to go to the library **but** he didn't know why.

6A. a. come in
   b. nervous
   c. answer
   d. begin
   e. antique
   f. open
   g. forget

h. lose
i. empty
j. dark
k. ill

B. a. I've always liked old furniture, how much is that **antique** chair?
   b. It's really hot in here, can you **open** the window?
   c. Matthew had to take antibiotics when he was **ill** last month.
   d. I'm not very lucky at playing cards, I always **lose**.
   e. Don't **forget** my birthday, it's tomorrow!
   f. Don't stay outside in the rain, **come in** and get dry.

7. a. Cranberry woke up one morning and decided he wanted to go to the **library**.
   He asked James, his **butler**, to drive him there in the Rolls.
   b. Cranberry was amazed to discover that Madame Eve knew everything about his **past**, his childhood, his girlfriends and his financial problems.
   c. When he arrived at the library, he went straight to the **librarian** and asked her for a copy of *Strange Destiny*.
   d. She also told him that his **luck** could be changed only by **burying** his heirloom in his **mother's** grave.
   e. The **visiting** card had an **address** in London that took him to see Madame Eve, a **clairvoyant**.
   f. When he opened the book a **receipt** fell out of it. It was from the local **pawnshop**.
   g. The **handle** of the mirror was loose and in it he found a **visiting** card.
   h. Cranberry went straight to the pawnbroker, gave in the **receipt** and **bought** a small, antique mirror.
   i. That **night** Cranberry took his great-**grandmother's** diamond necklace and buried it in the cemetery.

1.a	2.c	3.f	4.h	5.g
6.e	7.b	8.d	9.i	

THE PENFRIEND

Before reading (page 28)

1. Open answer.

2. Open answer.

After reading (page 46)

1. a. T
   b. F
   c. T
   d. F
   e. T
   f. F
   g. T
   h. F
   i. F
   j. T

   b. Susan replied a week later.
   d. Susan was doing well at school.
   f. Trudy did not receive any photos.
   h. Susan lied to the social worker.
   i. Susan had problems with her son and daughter-in-law.

2. awful; worried; police; mother; mother's; heard; letters; address; day; son.

3. a. If Trudy **goes** to the party, she'll have a good time.
   b. If I **call** the police, they'll contact the social services.
   c. The police will arrest them, if Trudy **tells** them about Susan.
   d. If you **write** to a British penfriend, you'll improve your English.
   e. If Trudy **doesn't go** to the party, Tony won't ask her again.

4. Dear Trudy,
   How are you? I'm sorry I **haven't written** to you for such a long time but I **have been** so busy since you **visited** me. By the way, thanks for the chocolates! My life **has changed** completely –
   I **have lived** here for two months now and I'm doing so many new things. I've started studying

French and also doing some travelling.
I **went** to Paris last week for a couple of days – it was very exciting! We **took** the ferry from Dover to Calais and then **caught** the train to Paris. I hope my French **has improved**!
That's all for now. Please come and visit me if you have time.
Lots of love.
Susan

5.-9. Open answers.

THE BIG MISTAKE

Before reading (page 52)

1. Open answers.

2A. a. Burglary: **to enter a house with the intention of stealing.**
b. Murder: **to kill illegally.**
c. Theft: **to steal.**
d. Robbery: **to steal from a bank.**
e. Shoplifting: **to take goods from a shop without paying.**
f. Kidnapping: **to take away a person and ask for money in return.**

B. murder   **murderer**
theft   **thief**
robbery   **robber**
shoplifting   **shoplifter**
kidnapping   **kidnapper**

After reading (page 66)

1.

8 h.   1 a.

3 c.   4 b.

2 d.   6 f.

2. Open answer.

3. a. Littlepoint
b. Potatoes
c. under the doormat
d. a quiz show
e. His slippers
f. 999
g. kitchen
h. 26
i. a mobile phone
j. some money
k. in the road
l. wine

4.

 5 e.   7 g.

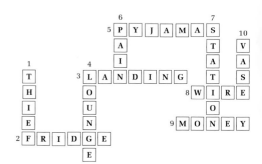

5. a. The fridge is nearly empty, **isn't it?**
b. Ian got off the train at Littlepoint, **didn't he?**
c. He didn't eat much, **did he?**
d. Ian likes watching quiz shows, **doesn't he?**
e. You're joking, **aren't you?**
f. The two men weren't thieves, **were they?**
g. That isn't blood, **is it?**

6. a. Ian came **by** train yesterday.
b. Ian **arrived** at Cliffview at about 6 o'clock.
c. Ian ate two boiled **potatoes, some ham** and drank **a bottle of** milk.
d. Ian tied the **man's hands.**
e. The two men turned **on** the light.
f. Ian chose the **biggest** room.
g. The thieves **cut** the outside wires.

7. a. off   **d. for**
  b. off   **e. up**
  c. down   **f. on**

8A.

hedge, grass, lawn, flowers, rosebush — **Garden**

telephone, coat, umbrellas, plants — **Hall**

shower, washbasin, bath, toilet, towels, toothbrush, toothpaste — **Bathroom**

cooker, fridge, freezer, microwave, dishwasher, sink, cupboards, plates, cutlery — **Kitchen**

bed, wardrobe, bedside lamp, chair, dressing table — **Bedroom**

television, bookcase, sofa, table, armchair, computer, carpet, cabinet — **Living room**

HOUSE

B. a. You usually cook in the **kitchen.**
b. Why don't you cut the **grass** in the garden?
c. I love watching **television** in bed.
d. The **wardrobe** in the bedroom is full of clothes.
e. British people usually hang up their coats in the **hall.**
f. My mother used to wash clothes by hand, I prefer using a **washing machine!**

9. a. You make a mistake.
b. You catch a train.
c. You pick up a suitcase.
d. You look at a watch.
e. You watch television.
f. You have a shower.
g. You hang up clothes.
h. You switch on the light.

10. Open answer.

Listening (page 75)

1. a. OK.
b. Ian was going to the sea.
c. OK.
d. Ian got off the train at Littlepoint.
e. He caught a taxi.
f. OK.
g. Ian went upstairs, took his clothes off and had a shower.
h. OK.
i. Ian ate his meal in the lounge.

2.

MARGE AND OLIVE

Before reading (page 78)

1. Open answers.

2. a. cow: the only word that is not used to describe meat.
b. coffee: the only one that is not a dairy product.
c. beans: countable noun.
d. cornflakes: not a drink.
e. pepper: vegetable.
f. cherry: fruit.

3. • crime
   • love

After reading (page 88)

1. a. Over 70.
   b. Olive.
   c. arthritis.
   d. cheese, milk, yoghurt.
   e. not mentioned.
   f. lost friends, dance halls, music of old days.
   g. chocolates, sweets, cream, yoghurt.
   h. fried eggs.
   i. She had a headache.
   j. heart attack.
   k. A few months after Olive's death.
   l. A tin of 'concentrated powdered milk'.

2. a. Marge and Olive's.
   b. Olive.
   c. clothes.
   d. cheese, cream, yoghurt.
   e. The fact that Alfred was accused of being a deserter.
   f. the letters.
   g. small tin and letter.
   h. egg.
   i. the letter.
   j. the label.

3. a. Marge met Alfred before the Second World War.
   b. Olive always read Marge's letters.
   c. Marge and Olive's father left a lot of money.
   d. Alfred had been accused of desertion.
   e. Marge hid the tin and the letter in her handbag.
   f. Marge picked up the telephone and called an ambulance.

4. 1.a   2.b   3.b   4.b
   5.b   6.c   7.b   8.b
   9.a   10.a   11.b   12.c

5. a. Marge was afraid **of** Olive.
   b. Olive was a little bit older **than** Marge.
   c. Olive liked going shopping **on** her own.
   d. Olive often talked **about** the price of clothes.
   e. Alfred asked Marge **to** marry him.
   f. Olive ordered Marge to make her a cup **of** tea.
   g. After a while Marge called **for** an ambulance.

6. At last Alfred and I **are** happy! Olive **died** last month and we had **her** funeral a week later. Now Alfred and I can get **married**. We **went** into town yesterday to do some shopping – I bought **myself** a beautiful pink dress and Alfred **bought** some new shoes. We hope to get married in a few **months'** time and then go to the seaside for **our** honeymoon. I sometimes miss Olive and her strange ways but I think I prefer to live with Alfred – he **loves** me so much ...

Listening (page 92)

1. a. Olive
   b. Marge
   c. Marge
   d. Alfred
   e. Marge and Alfred
   f. Marge
   g. Alfred
   h. Olive

2. Marge and Olive were two sisters who **had** lived together all **their** lives. They were both **over** seventy. When their father died leaving **them** the house and some money, it was Olive who was the boss. She was a **little** older than Marge and had a very bad **temper**. Marge was afraid of her, and soon **learnt** to do everything she was told to do. Olive did the shopping, paid the **electricity**, gas and water bills, and decided how to spend their money. Marge did the **cleaning**, the cooking and decided when to put the **rubbish** out to be collected.

SIMPSON'S BURIED TREASURE

Before reading (page 94)

1. Open answers.

2. a. **spade**: the only tool.
   b. **hot**: the only adjective.
   c. **cry**: the only verb.

3. a. Four.
   b. Nicholas, Buster, Driscoll, Lewis.
   c. A narrow country road.

After reading (page 104)

1. **a.** F
b. T
c. T
d. T
e. F
f. F
g. T
h. F
i. T
j. F

a. Nicholas met the boys in the narrow country lane.
e. Nicholas was running.
f. Nicholas hid behind a hedge.
h. Buster did not find anything.
j. She paid Nicholas for tidying up the garden.

2.

 a **3**

The boys **went** into the garden.

b **5**

Buster and his friends **started** working.

c **1**

Nicholas **met** Buster and his friends.

d **9**

Miss Simpson **gave** Nicholas some money.

e **2**

Buster **hit** Nicholas across the face.

f **6**

It started raining and Buster **fell** into a hole.

g **7**

The boys **left** the garden.

h **4**

Nicholas **hid** behind a hedge.

i **8**

Miss Simpson **arrived** in her car.

3. **a.** stupid   not very intelligent
b. legend   a very old story
c. spade   a tool used for digging
d. stumble   fall over
e. wet   not dry
f. yell   shout loudly
g. face   part of the body

4A. **a.** weeds
b. tool
c. lawn mower
d. spade
e. hedge
f. grass
g. rosebush

B.

G	D	R	R	S	T	Z	H	K
L	A	W	N	M	O	W	E	R
T	R	E	E	L	O	E	D	H
M	D	G	P	P	L	E	G	Q
U	X	R	S	P	A	D	E	V
D	Y	A	F	D	E	S	O	O
Y	U	S	Q	P	U	I	C	H
R	O	S	E	B	U	S	H	J

5A. **b.** colder   coldest
c. younger   youngest
d. richer   richest
e. fatter   fattest
f. hotter   hottest
g. wetter   wettest
h. thinner   thinnest
i. happier   happiest

j. smaller — smallest
k. better — best
l. worse — worst
m. more intelligent — most intelligent
n. more beautiful — most beautiful

B. a. He's **the fattest.**
  b. He's **the happiest and richest.**
  c. Lewis is **the tallest.**
  d. He's **the shortest.**

6.

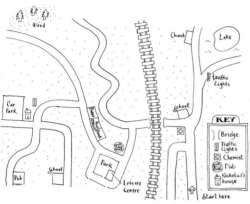

7. a. leg
  b. hand
  c. nose
  d. eyes
  e. mouth
  f. teeth
  g. feet / teeth
  h. ears
  i. chest
  j. neck
  k. forehead
  l. shoulders

Listening (page 113)

1. a. a map
  b. in a hedge
  c. Buster
  d. nothing
  e. windy
  f. £15

2. a. Buster
  b. Driscoll
  c. Miss Simpson
  d. Buster, Lewis, Driscoll
  e. Buster
  f. Nicholas
  g. Driscoll
  h. Miss Simpson

A STRANGE CASE

Before reading (page 116)

1. Open answers.

2. Open answers.

3. Possible words: man, men, oil, pin, lip, plan, line, pile, meal, leap, name, mean, mile, alone, police, clip, come, policeman.

After reading (page 125)

1. a. in the morning
  b. a chat
  c. lots of money
  d. near Perch's home
  e. a young boy
  f. Detective Galloway
  g. he had money problems

2A. a. daisies
  b. eyes
  c. men
  d. noises
  e. watches
  f. wives
  g. mice
  h. forks
  i. matches

B. a. children   **g.** jeans
  b. feet   **h.** rats
  c. women   **i.** pennies
  d. people   **j.** men
  e. teeth   **k.** knives
  f. trousers   **l.** glasses

3.

Adjective	Preposition	Verb
intelligent	towards	meet
his	into	chat
old	at	search
our	behind	wonder
	in front of	

Noun	Adverb
widower	hard
body	calmly
bread	helplessly

4.

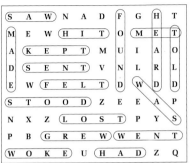

5.

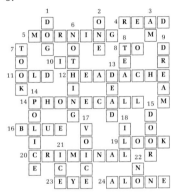

Listening (page 129)

1A. a. T
b. F
c. T
d. F
e. T
f. F
g. T
h. F

b. They talked about politics, the Second World War and the weather.
d. The thief also stole his wedding ring.
f. Marshall was not a friend of Mr Perch's.
h. Marshall choked on a piece of bread.

B. One day a man called Mr **Perch** came to see me in the police station. He had a very strange **story** to tell. He said he was going to be murdered very near in the future but he did not want me to look for his **murderer**. I told Marshall, another police officer, about the visit and then carried on working. The next **day** I heard that Perch was dead and that his money and wedding **ring** had been stolen. I started to look for the murderer with **Marshall's** help. **Three** days later I was with Marshall in my office – it was lunchtime and we were having a cup of **coffee** and eating some **sandwiches**. We were discussing Perch's case when Marshall said something that made me very suspicious. Suddenly he started **choking** on his sandwich. He died exactly how Perch had predicted – choking on a piece of **bread**.

TEST YOUR MEMORY (p. 131)

1. She did not get on with her parents.
2. Because his mother was ill.
3. The rosebushes in Miss Simpson's garden.
4. Detective Miller.
5. Two boiled potatoes, some ham and a bottle of milk.
6. By train.
7. She was changing the furniture.
8. She died of a heart attack.
9. A young boy.
10. Buster, Driscoll, Lewis, Nicholas and Miss Simpson.
11. Yoghurt, cream and chocolates.
12. His wife had appeared to him in a dream.
13. A mobile phone.
14. Rabbit.
15. Tony.
16. Early in the morning.
17. Over 70.
18. His great-grandmother's diamond necklace.
19. He choked on a piece of bread.
20. Four.
21. By taxi.
22. Red.
23. 10 Rosehip Lane, London SW6.
24. Marge's boyfriend.

A Case of Trust

a. False – Detective Miller wanted to see John Baker.
b. True
c. False – He asked the butler to take him to the library.
d. True
e. True
f. False – He put his great-grandmother's diamond necklace in his mother's grave.
g. True
h. False – Detective Miller got the promotion.

The Penfriend

a. False – She had to be home by ten o'clock.
b. True
c. False – Trudy's relationship with her parents got better.
d. False – She told her parents about Susan.
e. True
f. False – Susan was an old woman.
g. True
h. True

The Big Mistake

a. True
b. False – He ate only two boiled potatoes and some ham, and drank a bottle of milk.
c. False – He was worried and he trembled.
d. True
e. True
f. False – The number of his uncle's house was twenty-six.

g. False – The two men had run over a dog.

Marge and Olive

a. False – They were over seventy.
b. False – Olive was the boss.
c. False – Marge hated shopping days.
d. False – Olive always refused to buy these things for Marge.
e. True
f. False – Marge and Alfred planned to get married.
g. True

Simpson's Buried Treasure

a. False – Buster called him 'Rabbit'.
b. True
c. True
d. False – There wasn't any treasure buried in the ground.
e. True
f. False – Nicholas got paid for digging up the garden so well.
g. False – Nicholas received £15 from Miss Simpson.

A Strange Case

a. False – He was a tall man.
b. True
c. False – Mr Perch's body was found early in the morning.
d. False – The police detective tried to find the criminal.
e. False – The murderer choked on a piece of bread.
f. True